W9-AYP-597

AN AVALON ROMANCE

JUST BUSINESS
Kathy Attalla

Sensible Leah Matthews has always done what was expected of her. And while she has what she always wanted—professional success—she has the sinking feeling that life has passed her by. So while attending a marketing seminar in Hawaii, she decides to let loose a little. Jackson Brandt, a fellow hotel guest and gold medal runner, is more than willing to help her break out of her shell. He showers her with the kind of attention she rarely receives from men.

He seems like the perfect catch until she discovers that the company she works for has hired him and that she is his new boss. Her personal policy against inter-office romance and feeling of betrayal make for a tense working relationship. But memories of her romantic Hawaiian holiday won't allow her to keep him at a distance forever. Their sizzling chemistry and mutual respect make it hard for these star-crossed lovers to keep things at the company strictly business.

JUST BUSINESS

•

Kathy Attalla

AVALON BOOKS
NEW YORK

PRINTED IN THE UNITED STATES OF AMERICA
ON ACID-FREE PAPER
BY HADDON CRAFTSMEN, BLOOMSBURG, PENNSYLVANIA

For the wonderful members of Hudson Valley RWA
for their invaluable support.

Chapter One

Leah Matthews smoothed the silky material of her dress over her thighs. Dress? More like a glorified slip. Why had she let her cousin talk her into buying this? *Mutton dressed up as lamb*—that's what her very proper, British aunt would call her.

She pushed a handful of unruly curls off her shoulders. Sheer laziness had stopped her from blow drying the ringlets into her normal pageboy style, but now she wished she had. She shrugged. Who was she trying to impress, anyway?

Jackson Brandt lowered himself into the

chair next to hers. "I hope I didn't keep you waiting."

Their eyes met and her pulse rate accelerated—this was who she was trying to impress. She smiled. "No. I just arrived myself."

Customers in the quiet restaurant turned to stare. Leah guessed that was nothing new to her date. Jackson Brandt, an Olympic gold medal runner, had a lean muscular body and blue bedroom eyes that made him a focal point wherever he went. His khaki chinos and white short-sleeved shirt fit as if they were custom made for him. From the top of his chestnut hair to the soles of his Nike sneakers, he was the most perfect man she had ever seen, yet he seemed unaffected by his appearance.

She still couldn't believe she was having dinner with him, and for the fourth time in as many days. When she'd left for the conference, she had pictured long days in boring meetings, and evenings spent curled up with a good romance novel. As if her imagination had conjured him up from the cover of the book, Jackson had appeared from out of nowhere. Within moments he'd had her heart racing, and in only a few days he just plain had her heart. For the first time in her solid, predictable life she decided to give in to the fantasies she would never admit to having.

"Good evening," The waitress gazed at Jack. "Would you care for a drink?"

Unfortunately, Leah thought with an uncharacteristic blast of jealousy, *she wasn't the only woman admiring this man.* She might as well have been invisible, for all the interest the waitress showed her.

Jack, however, gave her his full attention. "Leah? What would you like?"

"A fruit smoothie."

His deep laughter warmed her. "Before we leave Hawaii, I'm going to get you to try a drink that isn't served in a piece of fruit."

Before they left Hawaii, she had a feeling that Jackson Brandt was going to get her to do a multitude of things that a woman—whose own staff called "Ice Queen"—would never dream of doing. The way he gazed at her brought a flush to her skin. And there was plenty exposed in her flimsy excuse for a dress.

Her fingers absently fidgeted with the spaghetti strap on her shoulder.

"You look gorgeous, Leah. Would you relax?"

Shyly, she lowered her hand to her lap and gave herself a smack. "I'm sorry. Sometimes I can't sit still for long."

"That's why you're so much fun."

Leah bowed her head. She was nearly thirty, yet he made her blush like an awkward teenager. "I think you enjoy embarrassing me," she muttered.

"Because it's so easy to do. You would think no man had ever flirted with you."

No one like him. Jackson was a mystery. He could have any woman in the hotel—heck, he could have any woman on the entire island with just a smile. Why was he falling all over *her*, as if she were the most fascinating woman in the world?

He made her feel beautiful, desirable—and suspicious. She didn't normally receive this kind of attention from men. Why couldn't she stop questioning her luck, and accept their relationship for what it was, a holiday romance?

"Leah?"

She shook her head to clear her skeptical thoughts. "I'm sorry. I'm a little distracted. I can't seem to leave my work back at the office." Which was a bold-faced lie. She hadn't thought about her job since she'd met him, except when he had asked her direct questions. Although he showed an enthusiastic interest in her career, she felt strange talking about herself all the time.

Jack leaned back in the wicker chair and focused on the hypnotic turquoise water. She was staring at him again. Not in the way most women did, seeing only the athlete, not the man. In fact, she was the first intelligent woman in a long time who had treated him as if he was something other than a dumb jock. His college degree notwithstanding, most people knew him only as an Olympic runner. He had come to the conference to network for a job in his chosen career of marketing, but it seemed many prospective employers weren't interested in his 4.0 grade average, since he had attended college on an athletic scholarship.

Leah was different. A shy beauty with brains. Oh, he knew her reputation. He had read several articles about her rise on Seventh Avenue. She was hailed as one of those twenty-something whiz-kids, a marketing genius who had taken a fledgling company, Rockford Industries, and turned it into a highly competitive powerhouse. He had introduced himself to the executive and had ended up captivated by the woman.

"It seems we're both distracted," Leah's gentle voice broke into his thoughts.

"Water has that effect on people." Before they could lapse back into their introverted silences, he reached for her hand. "Let's go for a walk."

"My drink . . ."

"We'll take it with us."

She glanced down at her flimsy blue dress. "Maybe I should run up and change first."

"Why?"

"I don't know. I feel restricted in this."

He laughed. "Any fewer restrictions and you'll be arrested." He didn't believe that women still blushed, yet for Leah the rosy flush seemed to come naturally.

He picked up the drink and met her at the water's edge. As if she had never experienced the feeling before, she pressed her toes tentatively into the wet sand. Often during the past few days he had wondered about her odd reactions to any kind of physical sensations, particularly intimate ones. Not that she feared intimacy, but she almost seemed unaccustomed to displays of affection. Any demonstrative gesture was a reaction to his action; she never initiated contact.

She turned to find him watching her. Her spontaneity slipped back under a rigid mask of control. She had a bit more trouble with her armor, as the hemline of her knee length dress swirled in a warm sea breeze.

"Here." He offered her the pineapple that contained her tropical drink. "Let's have a seat."

"There's only one lounge chair."

"You're an only child, aren't you?"

Puzzlement flickered in her emerald green eyes. "Yes. How did you know?"

"You don't know how to share." He slid his hand around her waist and pulled her down into the chair, fitting her snugly next to him.

Her fingers tightened around the pineapple, knuckles white with tension. She tried to wiggle forward. "You can't be very comfortable."

"Let me be the judge of that." He eased her against his chest, rocking her until she relaxed in the circle of his arms. Honey-scented hair brushed against his cheek. She felt good, all satin and warmth. That she was completely unaware of her beauty only added to her allure.

Leah sipped her drink. The sky over the Pacific turned to indigo as the sun dipped below the horizon. Nothing was real, not the colors, or the constant beat of the waves against the shore. Certainly not this man who unnerved her until she was a trembling mass of confusion. He was chaos in her neatly organized life.

Professionally, she had no trouble relating to men. On the other hand, her personal life had been less than successful. What did he want from her? "Jack?"

"Hmm?" he hummed in her ear.

"Why me?"

"Why not?"

"Well, look at me. I'm not exactly your type." He tensed, and she realized how shallow that made him sound.

"And what do you think my type is?" His voice held a trace of anger. Or was it hurt?

"I don't know. I'm just not sure I could be the kind of person you want."

"I don't want you to be someone else. I like being with *you*."

Since her arrival, he had been her constant

companion. Despite the blatant efforts of a few stunning women, he had never given more than a polite and short refusal to the offers. She had to stop questioning every one of his motives or she would drive him away. To her surprise, that was the last thing she wanted to do.

"So tell me about your job. Do you enjoy it?"

She had no interest in talking about the world of statistics and surveys and how they related to the fashion industry. "It's pretty boring stuff."

"Not to me. I have a degree in marketing."

"You do?" she exclaimed.

"What surprises you? That I studied marketing, or that I finished college?"

She closed her eyes and sighed. Luckily she had removed her sandals earlier, because she had just shoved her foot firmly into her mouth. Jack was smooth and eloquent, but she just assumed he had acquired his polish from the company he kept.

"Leah?"

"Give me a second. I'm choking on my foot." She took a sip of the cool drink and put the pineapple down in the sand.

"At least you're honest."

"I can't stomach a liar, so yes, I'm honest. Even when it gets me in trouble." A long silence followed. Had she insulted him? "I'm sorry."

He kissed the top of her head. "Don't be. Most people are surprised."

"I don't think it's meant personally. When you become known for something it isn't always easy for people to see beyond that."

"It's not as if I could make a career of running. Even the offers for product endorsements ran out eventually."

"It could be a difficult transition from the great outdoors to a desk job."

"Only if I'm not given a chance." His impassioned words touched a cord. She'd had to overcome similar obstacles when she had graduated from college at the tender age of nineteen.

"Well, you've certainly come to the right place to network for a job. You'll probably succeed if you put your mind to it. You have a very persuasive nature."

He had managed to draw her out of her shell. In the last two years she hadn't been on a date, let alone considered a relationship. She had a successful career, but something was missing from her life. Like a life. A shiver ran down her spine.

"Are you cold?" he asked.

Did cold feet count? "Not really."

She looked up and watched the stars spinning westward. Venus rose overhead, chased by a full moon. A perfect night for romance. She tipped her head back and brushed her mouth over his lips, tasting the lingering trace of salt.

Jack seemed to hesitate, as if surprised by the kiss. Was she wrong in assuming he was attracted to her? "Leah, I really need to talk to you about something first."

"Not tonight."

"I really think I should."

She slipped out of the chair and came to her feet. The undercurrents of anxiety in Jack's normally confident voice led her to believe that he didn't want to have this conversation on the beach where anyone could walk by and overhear. "You can walk me back to my room and then we can talk."

Jack followed Leah into her room. The television, blaring news blurbs via CNN, greeted them. "Sorry," she muttered and switched off the set. "A habit from living alone in the city. I hate coming home to a silent apartment."

Leah prowled around like a nervous feline. She rearranged the fresh flowers, fluffed the pillows on the love seat, and generally fidgeted with everything in her path. Her elegant suite, with a spectacular floor-to-ceiling view of the Pacific, must have cost three times what his had—a subtle reminder that this was a woman who had already made it in a business he was about to enter. In fact, if his interview with the owner of Rockford Industries went well tomorrow, he might be working in the same company.

"Would you like a drink or something?" Her uncertain smile gave her a natural beauty that most women could only wish to possess.

"*Or something* would be nice," he teased, just to watch her cheeks change to that delightful shade of pink again.

She turned and pressed her hands against the top of the white lacquer desk. "Okay," she said on the exhale of a ragged breath.

"I was teasing you. If I make you this nervous, it might be better if I left."

She whirled around and said, "No."

Apparently surprised by her own outburst, she sucked in a large audible gasp and stared straight down at the floor. "I mean, of course you can go if you wish. I mean . . ." She frowned, her voice trailing off to a whisper.

Where did her insecurity come from? The woman was beautiful, brilliant and successful. The she-cat of Seventh Avenue to the business world looked more like a timid kitten scanning the room for an escape.

Before she could dodge him, he caught her wrist and tugged her into his embrace. With his free hand, he pushed back the mass of curls from her cheek. "What's the matter?"

"I'm not good at this kind of thing . . ."

"Because it's not you, Leah. You're not ready." Perhaps it was just as well. He had a few things to discuss with her. By the time he finished, she might not even talk to him, let alone want to have a relationship with him. "How about we spend the day together tomorrow. I really need to talk to you about something."

"I already made plans for an island tour."

Although he could have probably convinced her to change her plans with very little persuasion, he remained silent. At least she would be able to take some happy memories back with her.

She smiled brightly. "I'll be back around four."

"Dinner?" he asked.

"How about we stay in and order room service?" she offered.

"Sounds good to me." He only hoped that by the time he explained his situation, he wouldn't be wearing the dinner over his head.

Jack stared at the tranquil water but felt no peace. He checked his watch. Only one more hour until Leah returned. He dangled the fishing pole in the water in a half-hearted attempt to pass the time. The wooden dock swayed from the pressure of the constant waves. The calm gave him too much time to think.

He should be pleased. His investment in this seminar had paid off. He got a bonafide job offer. Nice pay, good benefits. And Leah Matthews as his immediate boss. Just how was she going to take the news that Rockford's president had made an offer without first consulting Leah, as head of marketing? Should he have told her about his interview with the president of her company? Yesterday he had worried that telling her might give the wrong impression. Now he wondered if his omission might be worse.

He could turn down the job. If he had only himself to consider. However, he had obligations, and this was the first offer to come his way in a three-month search. Leah was a sweet, sympathetic woman. She would understand once he explained the situation.

Right! And the fact that you've been courting her this past week and now she's going to be your boss isn't going to bother her in the least, his conscience mocked back.

Shoving his hands into the pockets of his shorts, he headed back to the hotel. The sooner he told her about the job, the better.

"Room 215," he said to the desk clerk.

The man returned with his key and a message. Just when he thought nothing worse could happen, life had proved him wrong again. The short note from Leah explained that a family emergency had cut her trip short. Her sincere apology was written on her business card along with a quick, *call me if you'd like*, printed next to the phone number. Her business number! He couldn't get in touch with her before Monday to tell her.

Chapter Two

Leah stepped off the elevator on the twelfth floor. As she passed the break room, quite a few heads turned. The hushed whispers of office gossip followed. Normally, she wasn't a source of juicy rumors. Today, however, she expected to create a bit of a stir.

For the first time in years, she had overslept on a work day. With barely enough time to shower, she had let her hair dry in the natural, wavy fashion she had adopted in Hawaii. The more casual style clashed with her severe business suits, so she went with a floral print dress. The scoop neckline and full skirt were adequately modest, but she normally never showed up for work without her intimidation clothes buttoned up to her throat like a noose.

"Ms. Matthews?" Susan, her assistant, stared in wide-eyed wonder. Catching herself, the young woman shook her head and smiled ruefully. "You got sun stroke? I'm so sorry."

"Very amusing," Leah snipped. She reached for the stack of messages piled high in the memo bin. "Tell Randy I need to see him right away."

"Ellen brought in another one of her boy toys to work in . . ."

"I don't want to know."

"Weren't you at the same conference as she?"

"I didn't see her the entire time," Leah said as she stepped into her office. "Randy," she reminded Sue, before closing the door behind her.

So, Ellen Rockford was up to her old tricks again. Ever since Edward Rockford had died and his daughter had taken over the company, there had been a steady stream of young, good-looking men pushed into management positions. The company almost ended up with a lawsuit for passing over a more qualified female for Ellen's flavor of the month. Eventually, Leah might have to worry about her own job.

She smiled. While she knew more about the company than her employer, she was relatively safe. With ten years' experience invested in Rockford Industries, few people knew their products and market better than she did.

A light knock interrupted her thoughts. "Come in."

Randy Wilson entered and sat in the leather chair in front of her desk. "Leah?"

"No, I didn't suffer a severe blow to the head while away," she answered his unspoken question. She would have to get used to the gaping stares today.

"Well, I must say, Hawaii seems to have agreed with you."

She took Randy's comment as a friendly compliment since he knew better than to flirt with her. "Yes, it did." She couldn't quite stop the grin from spreading across her entire face.

"That good?" he asked.

"Never mind. Before I start answering these messages . . ." She indicated the large stack of pink slips covering the top of her desk. "I need to know if I missed anything important."

"Well, you already know about the manager Ellen hired at the seminar, since you were there. He starts today."

"Actually, I didn't know," she said as if she could care less. "And what will this one be managing?"

Randy's discomfort gave her a small clue, but she still felt a wave of shock when he said, "Marketing, under your direction."

"No." Her fist came down on the desk.

She thought she had made her position clear to Ellen before leaving. If the woman wanted to set up her own version of a harem, that was her business. She had neither the time nor the patience to deal with an egotistical pretty-boy who didn't know an asset from his . . . elbow.

"Look, Leah, I know you were against this. But you have to admit, the company has grown so much that you can't handle the day-to-day running of the business anymore. You're already handling more than your job description."

"And I said *if* and *when* I'm ready to take on a manager, I wanted to hire from within."

Randy shook his head. "You know that's

not a good idea. Management is usually brought in from the outside."

She knew, from a business standpoint, that he was probably right. But personally, she believed in rewarding company loyalty with more than a gold watch for twenty years of service. "Can this one at least read?"

Randy exhaled deeply. "I know him. We went to high school together. He has a good résumé."

If Ellen hired someone with practical knowledge, it would be the first time. "Experience?"

"He graduated from NYU at the top of his class."

"Experience?" she repeated.

"Not in the fashion industry," he grumbled. "But he's got an MBA in . . ."

"No experience?"

"Listen. Why don't you meet with him first and save your judgements for afterwards. He's with Ellen right now. They're waiting for you."

She would reserve judgement until she had a chance to speak with her boss. Then she would insist that Ellen find another position in the company for the *gentleman*. She rose and strode to the door, pausing to let Randy pass in front of her.

"One more thing," she said, halting his exit. "What's his name?"

"Jackson. Jackson Brandt."

Leah splashed cold water on her face. The feeling of nausea had passed, but after ten minutes, the shock was still as profound as when Randy had uttered the name. In a city of ten million people, odds were that more than one man was named Jackson Brandt. How many of them attended the networking seminar?

One, you idiot!

She felt the sting of salty tears filling her eyes and cursed herself—for crying, for caring, and most of all for trusting a man with her heart. A glance in the mirror confirmed her fear. She looked like a wreck and felt twice as bad. Well, Jackson Brandt had made a fool out of her once, but he wouldn't get the satisfaction of doing it again.

In a ritual born of habit, she quickly reapplied her make-up. Long ago, she had learned to channel her hurt. A childhood of taunting and cruelty, some of it at the hands of her own embittered father, had made her strong. At least, outwardly. A façade was all she needed.

Once her mask was in place, she stepped out of the ladies room. The walk down the long corridor was endless. She paused in front of Ellen's door and rapped her knuckles against the wall.

Ellen waved her in. "Here's our resident genius now."

Jackson rose from the chair. He had braced himself for a scene that never materialized—looking the epitome of poise, Leah strode in the office.

"Did you get mugged by a file clerk?" Ellen asked.

Leah smoothed the front of her dress and laughed, but he could tell she was not amused. "I got a late start today."

The older woman cocked an eyebrow suggestively. "Too much partying at the seminar?"

"Actually, it was quite boring." She glanced toward him. He thought for a moment that she was waiting for him to deny her charge. Returning her attention to her boss, she added, "You wanted to see me."

"Have a seat, both of you."

Jack sensed a tension between the two

women. He had learned from Randy that, despite the gold-leaf name plate on the door, Ellen Rockford was the president in name only. Leah Matthews was the real brains behind the success of the company.

"Leah, I'd like you to meet Jackson Brandt." Ellen sat in the chair behind the massive oak desk. Bleached blond hair was styled around her meticulously made up face. Apparently the woman did not intend to age gracefully. She had poured her well rounded body into a trendy navy suit, leaving her with little room to breathe.

Leah, on the other hand, possessed a natural beauty that a woman like Ellen would wholly resent. "I have a staff meeting at ten," Leah said.

Ellen nodded. "A task that you will no longer have to waste your time on. Now, I know you didn't want me to bring in a manager, but I felt, despite your objections, it was necessary. Jack came to us with an impressive résumé that even you would be hard pressed to find fault with, and a recommendation from Randy . . ."

At the mention of Randy's name, Leah flinched. In the split second before she recovered, her eyes reflected the full sense of her betrayal. If he didn't need the job so badly, he would have walked out the door just to prove he hadn't meant to use her.

Ellen continued with her speech. "Now you might argue that Jack lacks actual experience, but I seem to remember my father taking a chance on a green kid right out of college. You've done so well that our sales have increased ten fold. You can't carry it by yourself any longer." She paused as if waiting for a comment. "Leah?"

"Yes, Ms. Rockford."

"I'd like your input."

Leah stared at the floor. "You've already hired him. There's nothing to say."

"Well, that's settled." Ellen smiled, seemingly pleased with Leah's lack of argument.

He wasn't as easily fooled. Like a snow-capped volcano, deep in the center an inferno burned, waiting to erupt.

As if she couldn't leave fast enough, Leah sprung to her feet. "If you'll excuse me."

"While you're having your staff meeting, I'll take Jack under my wing and show him around," Ellen said.

"I'll bet you will," Leah mumbled under her breath. She raised her chin and walked out the door.

He watched her retreat with a frown. *What had she meant by her comment?*

"She'll cool off eventually. When my father was alive Leah got used to running things her way, but I'm not as easy to manipulate. I still own this company." Ellen pushed her chair back from her desk and crossed one leg over the other. Her skirt rose up to expose a nylon clad thigh. "I believe in encouraging new talent, and I'm going to take a personal interest in you."

The deliberately provocative gesture left him feeling like Dustin Hoffman being seduced by Mrs. Robinson. Now Leah's meaning became all too clear. How would he ever win her trust again if she believed he would use anyone to further his own ambitions?

Leah waited for Jack to enter her office, then closed the door. Her fury increased, threatening to explode in a violent rage. Twenty years to life. That was the penalty for murder, she reminded herself. Hardly a fair punishment for ridding the world of another rat. Unfortunately, in the eyes of the law, Jackson Brandt was a human being.

Remembering what had passed between them, her entire body flushed. How could she work with him day after day? Cowering be-hind him was a lousy way to start. She tugged up the neckline of her dress and walked around to her desk.

"Mr. Brandt."

"Jackson," he said and flashed her one of his smiles.

She didn't return the gesture. "Mr. Brandt. I'm sorry I haven't had time to review your résumé. As you are no doubt aware, I wasn't consulted before you were hired."

"Leah . . ."

"Ms. Matthews," she corrected.

"Leah," he said again in a voice that seemed barely controlled. "If you're going to fire me on my first day, I would prefer you get it over with so I can start looking for another job today."

She would like nothing better than to di-rect him to the nearest exit. Since Ellen hired him, she had no authority. "No, I'm not go-ing to fire you."

He leaned back in the chair. "Why?"

She grinned maliciously. "Because if you're not as good as you think you are, I'm going to enjoy watching you fall flat on your face."

"And if I am? Can I expect you to put a knife in my back?"

"I'd have to pull it out of mine first."

"Wait a minute." He came to his feet and pressed his hands onto the edge of her desk. His muscles filled the sleeves of his wool suit, testing the double stitching.

Concentrating on the wide expanse of his chest was too dangerous. She raised her head to glare at him. "You were saying."

"I wasn't trying to hurt you or damage your career in any way."

"Next you'll tell me that our meeting in Hawaii was a coincidence."

Did he take her for a complete fool? She thought back to all the things she had told him about herself and the company. Her policy had always been to keep her personal life private. She never indulged in office romance and discouraged it among her staff. If Jackson Brandt thought that wining and dining her would give him some sort of an advantage, he was about to get the kind of lesson they didn't teach in college.

"May I explain?"

She shook her head. "I don't want to hear it. Just do your job and stay out of my way."

"How do I do that? I work for you now."

"You work for Rockford Industries. When we need to discuss business, my door is open. If you want to relive the past, write your memoirs."

Jackson straightened and returned to his seat. What had he expected? Under the circumstances, she was more generous than he deserved. Buried beneath her hurt and anger, he remembered a loving woman afraid to follow her feelings. How could he blame her? With all her insecurities, he would never be able to convince her now that he hadn't intended to use her.

The only way to prove that his intentions had not been dishonest was by proving he could handle the job. He didn't want a free ride, only a chance.

"All right, Ms. Matthews. How do we begin?"

"I guess Randy can familiarize you with the accounts. Or has he already done that, too?"

Cheap shot, and one he fully deserved. "Look, I messed up and I accept responsibility for that. Randy suggested the seminar to network for a job, but that's all."

"I don't want to discuss it. And I would appreciate it if you would do the same."

He hadn't lost his job, but he sadly acknowledged that he had lost something far more valuable. Her trust.

She shuffled the papers on her desk. The gulf between them widened in the silence. "Have you been down to personnel to fill out the tax and insurance forms?"

"Not yet."

"Then maybe you should take care of that first. When you're settled in your office, I'll introduce you to the staff." She switched on her computer terminal. Her fingers pounded the keyboard, drumming her anger in a staccato rhythm. "Was there something else?"

Her dismissal was as cold as the stares she sent him. He might have to pull his parka out of winter storage if this icy barrier between them remained. He stood and managed a smile. "Thank you."

"Save it."

He took a step toward her desk. "Leah . . ."

"You got what you wanted. Quit while you're ahead."

"What is it you think I wanted?" he asked.

"You wanted to make sure I didn't voice my objections to your being hired, and I didn't." She lowered her head and hid her eyes behind the veil of soft curls. "Look at the bright side. At least I got called home before you actually had to go any further with me. I hope spending time with me wasn't too much of a hardship on you."

He felt as if he'd been kicked in the gut. "That was the best thing that ever happened to me."

"You're young yet. I'm sure if you work at it, you can humiliate a few more women in your lifetime."

"That wasn't my intention."

"Well, that was the result." As if trying to fight off a headache, she pressed her fingers against her temples.

"I'm sorry."

She wiped the back of her trembling hand across her cheek. "Would you please leave?"

As he walked out of the office, he pretended not to notice that she was crying. Not because he wanted to, but because that was the kindest thing he could do. He never meant to hurt her, but then, he never meant to fall for her either.

Jack stepped off the bus. Indian summer couldn't warm the chill he felt in his heart. As he walked through the suburban neighborhood, the events of the day refused to wind down. The marketing department hadn't extended a rousing welcome, which came as no great surprise.

Leah had given them all the right speeches about team work and being helpful, but the undercurrent of resentment had choked the office atmosphere. Her staff was devoted to her. They viewed his presence as an intrusion and possibly even a threat to their boss.

"Heads up."

Jack dropped his briefcase just in time to catch the football spinning toward him.

His brother, Tim, smiled sheepishly. "Nice catch."

"Lousy kick."

Tim shrugged. "So, Mr. Executive. How was your first day at work?"

"Not bad," he lied.

"Does that mean that they didn't *can* you?" Tim asked.

"No, they didn't."

"Oh, good. Now that we have medical insurance, does that mean I can go out for the football team?" As with all fifteen year olds, his brother only concerned himself with the bottom line. What was in it for him?

"Thirty days until the insurance kicks in."

Seeing the disappointment on Tim's face, he relented. "I suppose I could get private insurance for one month."

"Thanks. I want to call the coach."

Jack picked up his briefcase and followed Tim back to the house. Since his parents were killed by a drunk driver eight years ago, he had been his brother's guardian. Although his aunt had offered to take them in, Jack had refused. An athletic scholarship had paid his college tuition. The Olympic medal brought a few endorsements that had paid the bills on their house. Money was scarce for the most part, so Tim had missed out on many of the small things that most of his classmates in the middle-class neighborhood took for granted. Even simple sports were denied when the school found out they had no medical coverage. For his brother's sake, he needed a job with a regular income and benefits. Still, he couldn't help but feel guilty about the length he had gone to achieve that goal.

Chapter Three

Leah tossed her purse down on the kitchen counter. A throbbing pain pierced her temple. She had a giant headache, and it had Jackson Brandt written all over it. Ten minutes and two aspirin later, her nerves finally began to settle to the level of merely agitated.

Tomorrow she would send Aunt Mary a thank you note. When her hypochondriac of an aunt had called her home from Hawaii for an emergency that turned out to be a case of indigestion, she had wanted to shoot the woman. Now, she was grateful. If she had stayed the weekend, she might have made an even bigger fool of herself.

After changing into her flannel bathrobe and slippers, she settled onto the sofa to watch the news. Absently, she rubbed her chest. Now she knew why they called it heartache.

The searing pain couldn't be worse if he had sliced her with a knife. How could she have been so stupid? Only this morning she had imagined herself in love with him, and had even deluded herself into believing he might feel the same. She should have known that any man that easy on the eyes had to be hard on the heart. Her beautiful dream had become a nightmare. He didn't care about her. He had used her to gain information about the company.

Swallowing hard, she held back a flood of tears. She would not cry over Jackson Brandt again. Instead she turned her mind to more important matters. It was time to update her résumé. Over the years she had received quite a few offers to leave Rockford Industries. Her youth and her self-doubts had prevented her from making the leap to a larger company. Now Rockford *was* one of those larger companies, due in part to her abilities.

Any debt Leah owed to her mentor, Edward Rockford, had long been paid. Ellen didn't want to learn how to run the company, she wanted to use it as her own private escort service. For too many years Leah had turned a blind eye to Ellen's outrageous behavior because of all that Edward had done for her. Those days were over.

Having reached this conclusion, Leah felt instantly better. She no longer had to guard her words with her boss. If Ellen fired her before she found another position, she had enough savings to tide her over. The decision to leave afforded her more power and freedom than ten years with the company ever had.

Let Jack have her job. He might have a degree in business from a prestigious university, but some things couldn't be learned from a book. Just because he had been hand-picked as her replacement didn't mean he could fill her leather pumps.

Leah glanced at her watch. "Sue, call Mr. Brandt and see what's keeping him."

This had been one of the longest weeks on record. Her staff attributed her lethargic mood to PMS. Thankfully, they didn't suspect the truth. Working with Jackson, even being in the same room with him posed a distraction she couldn't seem to ignore.

The memories themselves were hard enough to relive. Knowing that he shared those memories made her want to run and hide—which was precisely why she stood and fought. She had never given into her fears, and he wouldn't make her start now.

"He's on his way," Sue said. Her smug grin was reflected on the faces of the four other people in the room.

Had she unfairly biased her department against Jack? Leah shook her head and wondered why she cared.

In less than a minute he entered the conference room. His eyes reflected his confusion. "I'm sorry. I wasn't aware there was a meeting this morning."

"You should have received a memo with the target reports. Sue, you did send a copy to Mr. Brandt, didn't you?"

"I'm sure I did. Perhaps it got mislaid somewhere in his office." One look at her assistant's smug expression and Leah knew that the reports would certainly turn up in his office, though they hadn't been there on time.

She waited, expecting Jack to make some

comment on the oversight. With all eyes in the room on him, she imagined that he felt uncomfortable. He only shrugged.

"We'll postpone this meeting until this afternoon," Leah said to the others. "Three o'clock."

As the room cleared out, she caught hold of Sue's arm to prevent her from leaving. Waiting until the others were out of earshot, she turned and said, "I don't want that to happen again."

Although she appreciated the sentiment, she could not tolerate a deliberate attempt to sabotage Jack. Her victory would only be sweet if he buried himself.

"If we make him look bad he'll be history before the Christmas party." Sue beamed as if her plan was brilliant.

"It doesn't work that way. If he's incompetent, he'll make himself look bad."

"And if he isn't?"

"Then he's doing his job. That improves our efficiency rating, and the end result is reflected in the sales." She couldn't believe she was sticking up for Jack. In truth, she admired the fact that he didn't place blame for the oversight. "You owe him an apology."

"What?" Sue exclaimed.

"If the situation were reversed I would make him do the same. This isn't kindergarten."

"Are you suggesting that I behaved like a child?"

Leah arched her eyebrow. "If the shoe fits . . ."

As she reached for the door handle, the young woman shook her head. "I can't believe you're defending him. He's already got the Ice Queen on his side. And you know what that means."

With a grunt of annoyance, Leah slammed the door. Although Ellen had been keeping a discrete distance for the past week, eventually the Black Widow would entice Jack into her web. Her stomach muscles constricted but she convinced herself that hunger rather than jealousy had caused the uncomfortable feeling.

Jack skimmed through the reports. He would have preferred more time than his lunch hour to study the results of the survey. Oversight, his foot! The woman had gone out of her way to make him look bad. The first letter he asked her to type for him had no less than six spelling mistakes. Did they think he couldn't read?

There seemed to be a collective effort among the department to undermine his authority. Memos appeared at the last minute, his questions received vague answers. The worst, however, were the personal digs.

One more dumb jock comment and he wouldn't be held responsible for what happened. Yes, it took him six years to finish college, but that was because he'd had to take two years off to train for the Olympics. Without the money he made in endorsements, he wouldn't have been able to pay the mortgage while he finished college.

"May I come in?"

He looked up to find Leah leaning against the door frame. Her glorious mane of ringlets was confined in a severe bun. With the exception of his first day, she always wore a muted color business suit. She put as much effort into appearing invisible as most women put into standing out. Would she ever again be the woman he had known in Hawaii? Her attitude toward him had not thawed one degree, but at least her dealings with him were honest and to the point.

"I'm almost finished going over this report."

She stepped inside and closed the door. "Don't bother. I've rescheduled the meeting for tomorrow morning."

"That wasn't necessary." He refused to let her think he couldn't handle the pressure.

Not even a hint of a smile touched her full lips. "It was. We have to attend a meeting with the advertising people this afternoon."

He cocked his eyebrow. "We? I'm surprised you've included me."

"I'm not asking you on a date. It's important that you attend, since you'll be dealing with them in the future."

Judging by her expression, she would rather submit to elective surgery than hand over one small part of her authority to him. How long would the wall remain between them?

"What time?" he asked.

"Two. I'll meet you in the lobby."

"I'll be ready." She turned to leave. "Leah?"

"Yes?"

At least she didn't snap at him for addressing her by her first name. Perhaps she was warming up, but he didn't expect a miracle.

A glacier couldn't melt overnight. "Did you have lunch?"

"Excuse me?"

"Lunch. Did you eat?"

"I usually don't."

"Well, would you care to share mine while you fill me in on the promotion?" He pointed to the brown bag on his desk and arched an eyebrow invitingly. "Turkey on rye with mayo."

She seemed to hesitate slightly before shaking her head. "You've read up on the account. You don't need my input."

"Oh, but I do."

"If you've got a question, ask. If not . . ." Her voice trailed off as she reached for the handle.

"I understand. You're afraid."

"Of you?" she asked incredulously.

The man needed his ego taken down a peg. Unfortunately she couldn't think of a clever retort to put him in his place, and she wouldn't if she could. The corners of her mouth turned down. Destroying self-confidence wasn't her style. Having grown up with a father who had mastered the art of humiliating his daughter, she knew all too well how that felt.

"Then have a seat and help out the new kid on the block."

She nodded. He might be the new kid, but he had been around the block a few more times than she had. Curiosity kept her from leaving. She hoped to discover what he still wanted from her, and how far he would go to get it.

He pushed half of his sandwich across the top of the desk. She wouldn't have figured him the brown-bag type. Power lunches at the popular bistro across the street were the norm for the office personnel.

"Well, sit down. I don't bite," he said.

No, he kissed, and she remembered that. At the time, she had liked it. A tingle danced down her spine. Angered by her body's traitorous response, she snapped up the sandwich and bit into the soft rye bread.

She lowered herself into the chair next to his desk. "So, what do you want to know?"

"I guess I'm curious about the kind of promotion you give each line. What percentage of the budget do advertising, publicity and sales promos make up? What is the target market? Are the ads slanted toward that market?"

His thirst for knowledge surprised her.

"Whoa. One at a time. The budget figures are in the computer."

Resentment darkened his eyes to a midnight blue.

"Which my personal ID number won't allow me to access. About the only thing I can bring up are the games, unless I use Randy's number, and even his access is limited."

"Did it ever occur to you to ask, instead of being so stubbornly independent?"

He met her gaze. "Yes it did, but then we both know what a fine group of team players we have in our department. Unfortunately, they seem to think I'm on the opposing side."

The warmth of embarrassment spread across her cheeks. He probably thought that Sue had acted on her orders. "What happened today won't be repeated. For now you can use my number."

She took another bite of the sandwich while he gave the number a try. After two short beeps he had full access to all of Rockford's files.

"I appreciate that." He grinned, and an unexpected surge of happiness pulsed through her.

Had she learned nothing? One smile and he had reduced her to a quivering blob of

Jell-O. Her body might have short term memory, but her emotions were still raw from the experience. So why did her heart still insist on beating in double time?

". . . your birthday?" Jack said.

Leah shook her head. "What?"

"You have a birthday coming up in a couple of weeks."

She drew her eyebrows together in thought. Had she told him her birthday? Not likely, she thought, since she wanted to deny the event herself. "How did you know?"

"Your ID number. Most people use their birthday so they won't forget."

"Oh. Well, that used to be my birthday, but after twenty-one, I gave them up. I heard they could shorten your life span."

In spite of the fact that she was half-serious, he chuckled. "Did anyone ever tell you you're funny?"

"No." She had been called many things, some flattering, some insulting, but funny had not been among them.

"Perhaps if you laughed more. I miss that about you."

The conversation had become too personal for comfort. "I really have to go. I have a few things to take care of before we leave for the meeting."

She jumped to her feet. The forward motion propelled her into the corner of the desk. With a muttered swear, she rubbed the sore spot on her hip, stepped back and almost tripped over the chair. Jack rose to help her but she waved him off. Gathering as much dignity as she could, she steadied herself and walked to the door.

"The rest of your sandwich . . ." he called after her. Was she paranoid, or did his voice hold a trace of laughter?

"Forget it. The way I'm going, I'd probably drop it down the front of my blouse."

This time, there was no mistake—he was laughing at her.

Well, her turn would soon come. When Ellen began to strut him around like a trained poodle, she would split her sides with laughter.

The meeting ran longer than Leah had anticipated. As much as she hated to admit it, Jack's probing and prodding probably saved them a bundle in cost overruns. The ad people couldn't slip one unaccounted cent past him without question.

Once they were in the taxi, Jack turned to her. His broad grin left her with no doubt that she was once again the source of his amusement.

"What?" she asked, while checking to make sure she hadn't spilled hors d'oeuvres down the front of her suit.

"I appreciate your support, but I didn't realize you were a football fan."

Her fingers clenched around the leather briefcase.

"Meaning?"

" 'You don't take the quarterback out of the game when he's scoring touchdowns'?," he quoted an earlier statement she had made.

What was his problem? She had let him handle Samuels, when it was obvious that the slick ad man would have preferred to deal with her. "And?"

"And, nothing. I liked the analogy, but it surprised me. I got the impression you wanted me permanently benched."

She shrugged. "My personal feelings have nothing to do with business. I'm smart enough to hand over the ball to someone who knows more than I do on a specific subject."

"I never meant to imply that you weren't

smart." Exasperation caused his voice to raise. "I didn't think you trusted me."

"I don't. But I trust that you'll do what's best for the company."

"Then do you think you could relax a little? I wasn't criticizing, I was trying to pay you a compliment."

Criticism was what she had been conditioned to expect in life. Compliments she had never learned to accept gracefully. "Why?"

He raised his shoulders in a gesture of defeat. "I'm beginning to wonder myself. No matter what I say, it's going to be wrong."

Guilt washed over her, but she had no idea why. After what he'd done, could he honestly believe she would let down her guard again?

Still, she couldn't fault him on his work. More than any other of Ellen's *finds*, Jack was technically qualified for the position for which he'd been hired—a fact she found both irritating and surprising. Smart and handsome was a combination not easily ignored.

The trip back to the office seemed endless in the rush hour traffic. She welcomed the smoggy, humid air as she exited the taxi. At least the choking smells of the city erased the musky scent of Jack that had filled the close confines of the back seat.

A flood of people stepped out of the elevator into the lobby, nearly trampling them in their rush to begin the weekend. During the ride up, they had the elevator to themselves. She leaned against the wall and closed her eyes. One week and she had survived without cracking. Next week could only get better.

"Do you feel all right?"

Her eyelids fluttered open. *Darn! Why couldn't he be old, ugly and obnoxious?* "Just resting. I have a long night ahead."

"A date?"

Her imagination must be working overtime. She would almost swear he sounded jealous. No, she decided. He would have to care about her to feel that kind of emotion. "Sure. With the man of my dreams."

"Leah?" He stroked his fingers along her arm.

Awareness of him heightened all her senses. A wide range of emotions ran through her, but she focused on her anger and pushed his hand away.

"What I do is none of your business." The

elevator came to a stop. She took a step forward and, as soon as the doors slid open, bolted for her office.

With a frustrated yelp, she threw herself into the chair behind her desk. So much for her brilliant plan to ignore him. Her body refused to cooperate. Too bad no one had come up with a cure for getting over a man.

She picked absently through a pile of junk mail. One advertisement brought a smile. *Relieve stress and improve your cardiovascular system through belly dancing.*

"Oh, right," she muttered and tossed the paper in the garbage.

After forty-five minutes of trying to concentrate on the sales figures, Leah switched off the computer. What was wrong with her? She used to enjoy sitting around the office after everyone had gone, but today it only served to remind her that she had no one to go home to.

Perhaps a movie would lift her dreary mood. She gathered her purse and jacket from the small closet. On her way out the door, she paused at her desk.

"Go on, you coward. You know you want to," she chided herself. Before she could change her mind, she pulled the flyer from the garbage can and stuffed it in her pocket. At this point, a little cardio-vascular activity couldn't hurt.

Chapter Four

"Is it all right if I throw a beer party and trash the house?" Tim asked.

Jack plunged his fork into a plate of spaghetti. "Not if you want to live to see your sixteenth birthday."

"Just wanted to see if you were listening."

"I'm listening. I just have a lot on my mind."

Since Jack had returned home, Tim had been talking non-stop. Hearing the trials of a love-struck teenage boy only underscored the point that things didn't get better with age. He had his own troubles, and the situation wasn't likely to improve soon.

51

"Are you having problems with your boss?" Tim asked.

Problems? "No. She's very polite to me." So polite he'd like to goad her into taking a swing at him—at least she would get the cold anger out of her system.

"If you're not going to finish that spaghetti, can I?" So much for Tim's sibling concern.

Jack pushed the plate across the table. He had no appetite. Leah's parting words bothered him more than he cared to acknowledge. Did she claim to have a date out of spite, or was she seeing someone?

The kitchen door opened as Tim said, "Oh, I forgot to tell you. Randy's coming over."

"Nice going, Drip." Randy sat in a chair at the table and took a piece of bread.

"Don't call him names," Jack said, then turned to his brother. "And if you're finished, you can go to the park. Be back by nine."

"Nine?" Tim complained.

"Eight-thirty," Jack countered.

"Nine." Tim ran out the door.

Jack cleared the table and loaded the dishwasher. He felt dead-tired. Eventually, he would get used to the routine, but the first week of commuting was a killer.

"So, how do you like working for the Ice Queen? Is it chilly in the marketing department?" Randy asked.

It was an Arctic freeze, but he wasn't about to admit that to his friend. "She's got a brilliant mind. I can learn a lot from her."

"Her looks ain't bad either, but you can forget about getting anywhere with her."

Jack grinned. "I guess that means you've tried. You say that about every woman who turns you down."

Apparently Randy's ego didn't take well to the refusal. He grabbed a soda from the refrigerator and flopped down in a chair. "Well, excuse me. You wouldn't know what it's like to be turned down."

"Don't be so sure. Anyway, she's a lot easier to take than that barracuda who owns the company."

"What do you mean?"

Jack grimaced. "I think Ellen was making a play for me."

"And?" Randy asked, obviously interested in the outcome.

"And what? I ignored it."

Randy's eyes expanded double width. "Are you crazy? You could be running the marketing department in six months if you play your cards right, and then I could work for *you*."

"Oh, right!" Jack snapped. "Like Ellen Rockford can afford to lose Leah. The woman couldn't run the company without her."

"Not right now, and don't think that isn't a sore point with our esteemed president. She hates Leah, but she needs her. Since Ellen's ex-husband left the company, anyway," Randy explained. "She was married to Marcus Chatsworth."

"The owner of . . ."

"Mercury Sportswear. Yeah, he bought into the company with the huge divorce settlement he got from Ellen—all because she couldn't remain faithful. Five years later, Chatsworth is her biggest competitor."

"How do you know all this?"

"Megan, over in receivables. She's got a crush on me. She told me that's how Mike Walsh got into the accounting department. His administrative assistant is real smart, but he never took a business course in his life. He'll just play along until Ms. Rockford finds a new *hobby*."

Jack raked his fingers though his hair. "Are you serious?"

"Why not? You didn't seem to mind when it came to those endorsement accounts. If I looked like you, I'd cash it in for all it was worth."

He never noticed Randy's resentment of him before. Was that the reason his friend hadn't warned him about Ellen before he applied for the position? Or did Randy think he would play up to the wolf in high heels to further both their careers? The thought made him ill. "I think I'd rather stay in middle management."

"You'll never get rich like that. You'll have to rent out the basement apartment of your house again."

"I'll manage." His parents had converted the lower floor into an apartment for his grandparents when he was growing up. To make ends meet while in college, Jack had rented the place, but after having a few unruly tenants, he swore he would find some other way to pay the bills.

Randy shrugged, apparently thinking Jack had made a huge mistake. "Do you want to go down to the pub and check out the action?"

"You go. I'm not in the mood."

The only action he wanted to check out

was going on somewhere in New York. He couldn't get Leah out of his mind. Thinking that she might be with some other man nearly drove him out of his mind.

"You've been a real bore ever since you got back from Hawaii," Randy grumbled.

"Then why not call Megan from receivables?"

"And break Ms. Matthew's cardinal rule against interoffice romances? That right is reserved for Ellen Rockford alone."

Leah wiped the sweat from her forehead. She never imagined that belly dancing would be so exhausting, or complicated. The small class of four made for personalized attention and a strenuous work out.

Her teacher, Madam Justine, had to be close to sixty but she moved with a grace Leah could only hope to possess. The older woman tucked a lose strand of grey hair into her bun as she watched Leah try to duplicate her movements.

"No, no, no," Madam Justine said in her delicate Greek accent. "Rotate the hips slowly while keeping the feet flat and slightly apart."

Leah sighed. No wonder she couldn't catch on.

"Try again."

"If I do that, I'm afraid it will look more like slam dancing," Leah let out through her frustration. Her fellow students were still laughing when the class ended.

Madam Justine touched her arm. "You wait, please."

She tensed, sure the teacher would tell her she was hopeless. Her muscles ached, and she bent over to massage the tightness in her legs. She braced herself for the worst and straightened. "Yes?"

"I think perhaps you might like to borrow a tape so you can practice from home. I sense you will not let go with the others around."

"Am I that obvious?"

"Well, dear, you are a bit . . ." Madam Justine paused as if searching for the correct word. ". . . stiff. But you found the courage to join the class. I think you are just the kind of person who can not loosen up until you are sure you can succeed."

Leah agreed with her teacher's assessment. Risk had never been a word in her vocabulary. She found comfort in routine. The fear of failure had stopped her from trying anything new.

Her mind drifted back to the disastrous results the first time she had done something out of character. Facing Jack at work each day, she wasn't even allowed to forget.

Ellen Rockford pressed her palms against the edge of the desk and leaned forward. "How have you been settling in?" she asked.

Jack pushed his chair back from the desk before her perfume consumed the last breathable air in the room. "Fine."

"Leah tells me you gave the advertising people a run for their money last week."

He hid his surprise. Leah had actually paid him a compliment? "Just doing my job."

Ellen smiled, showing off her straight capped teeth. "I knew I made the right choice when I hired you. I'm a very good judge of character." Her praise would mean a lot more if she looked him in the eye instead of checking out the rest of him while she spoke. "I hope Leah hasn't been too difficult."

"Not at all." At least not where work was concerned. Anything else, he deserved.

"Well, if you have any problems with her, come see me."

"I doubt that will be necessary."

A knock on his door answered his prayer. Ellen straightened and stepped away from his desk.

Leah strolled in the office and stopped dead. Her fingers tightened around the papers in her hands. She gazed at Ellen, then at him. From the expression on her face, she wasn't pleased with what she witnessed. "Ms. Rockford. I didn't realize you were here. I'll come back later."

Ellen's suggestive smile seemed more for the benefit of Leah than him. "We can pick this up later. I wouldn't want to interfere with his work." With a backward wave, she slipped out of the office.

Jack groaned. Ellen had deliberately left Leah with the impression they were discussing something other than business. Just what he needed. One more problem that required damage control. "What can I do for you, Leah?"

Her forced smile couldn't hide the anger reflected in her eyes. "The new figures came in from costing and I wondered if you had time to go over them now."

He glanced at his watch. For the better part

of the week she had avoided him whenever possible. Now that she asked for his help, he couldn't stay. "Can it wait until tomorrow?"

"Tomorrow is Saturday. Never mind—I wouldn't want to upset your evening plans. I'll take care of it myself."

"I don't mind giving up my Saturday." Even as he made the offer, he knew she would stay tonight and work on the account alone. "I have to go to a football game. It's opening night. Why don't you come with me and we can go over the reports afterwards."

"Excuse me?" Although she understood what he had said, she couldn't believe he had asked her. A football game? She exhaled a sigh of relief, then cursed herself. Why was she relieved to discover that he didn't have a date, as she had assumed?

"Well, you have to eat. I'll buy you a hot dog."

She hadn't gone to a football game since college. Would it really hurt to get out of the office for a few hours? She had been under a lot of stress lately.

Of which Jack was the primary cause, she reminded herself.

"I want one of those big pretzels too," she added before she could stop herself.

"Did you accept?"

"As long as you understand, it's not a . . ."

"Date, I know. It's a business dinner. I'll submit the receipt for reimbursement."

He smiled and she wondered what she had done. Around Jack her brain ceased to function and her heart took over. A part of her wanted to strangle him but the other part wanted to lose herself in his strong embrace. No wonder she was in such a state of confusion.

"Jack, maybe this . . ."

"Let's go or we'll miss the opening kick off." He rose and grabbed his briefcase before she could back out.

"May I stop to get changed first?"

"If it doesn't take more than five minutes. The game is over in Jersey."

She didn't have time to make the trip uptown to get clothes, so she decided to wear the black leggings and sweatshirt she kept in the office for her dance class. Being a coward, she used the ladies room in the lobby to change, so she wouldn't be seen by her coworkers. In less than her allotted five minutes she was ready to leave.

* * *

Leah waited in the backyard while Jack went inside. The split level house in the New Jersey suburb took her by surprise. She had assumed that he lived in one of those condominium complexes along the Hudson River. The trees shimmered in streaks of red, orange and gold against the western sun. She sat in an Adirondack chair and closed her eyes. How different from her brownstone in Manhattan, where the only time foliage rustled was when the neighbor's cat landed in her ficus tree.

At the sound of approaching footsteps, she peaked out through half closed eyes.

"Wake up, Sleeping Beauty."

She exhaled her exasperation at his comparison. "Wrong on both counts. I'm not sleeping, and I'm no beauty."

"I'm entitled to my opinion." He held out his hand and pulled her to her feet. "Do you feel like walking or would you rather I drive?"

"Let's walk," she said, and waited for him to lead the way.

After a day behind a desk, the half mile stroll to the school through the quiet town felt heavenly. Crowds formed at the entrance to the football field. Jack shot her a glare as she tried to pay for her own ticket.

"Do you always come to the high school games?" she asked, once they had gotten inside.

"This year I will."

"Oh, why is that?"

He took her arm and led her toward the fence. "There's someone I want you to meet."

The hometown Cougars were already sitting on the benches awaiting the coin toss. A young boy, sporting shoulder pads that bolstered his thin frame, jogged toward them.

"Hey, Jack, I guess the *Dragon* let you out early." He glanced toward Leah and his blue eyes widened. "Who's the babe?"

She choked back a laugh at Jack's bug-eyed stare and offered her hand. "I'm the Dragon. Who are you?"

The boy flushed and lowered his head. "Oh, no."

"My brother, Tim," Jack said tersely. He punched Tim's shoulder pads. "Show some respect to my boss."

"Oh, please," she said, feeling quite flattered by the compliment. "Any guy under the age of twenty-one who calls me a babe will be forgiven anything."

Jack arched one eyebrow hopefully. "What about one over twenty-one?"

"He gets a kick in the shins."

Tim grinned shyly. "I'm really sorry, but Randy sort of described you differently."

Leah nodded. "I'm sure he did. But I generally refrain from breathing fire in public places."

"Did I get you in trouble?" Tim asked his brother.

"Not any more than I was in before you opened your mouth."

Tim returned to his team, leaving Jack at an uncustomary loss for words. What was he worried about, she wondered? By this point, it came as no surprise that Randy had been less than kind in his description of her. Ironically, she had believed they had a good working relationship. Or maybe not so ironic—her judgements concerning men had not proven accurate.

She leaned against the fence and scanned the crowds filling the bleachers. "Are your parents here, too?"

"They were killed by a drunk driver eight years ago. It's just Tim and me."

"I'm sorry."

"It was a long time ago." He shrugged, then smiled wryly. "Unless my poor orphan status will win me any brownie points."

She laughed. "Not in this life."

"Well, what would it take?"

She pushed off the chain link fence and drew herself up to full height. "The days of me being impressed by you are long gone." *Stop lying to yourself Leah. You've been impressed since the first moment you laid eyes on him.*

"Then why did you agree to come this evening?"

"I like football."

"And that's the only reason?"

"Yep." That, and a few other personal reasons she wasn't ready to own up to.

The corner of his mouth lifted in a cocky grin. "You want to know what I think?"

"No. But I'm sure you'll tell me anyway."

"I think that despite everything, you still like me and you resent me for it."

She shook her head. "You're wrong. I care for you. And I hate myself for that."

So much for not admitting her personal reasons. She turned and walked toward the hot dog stand so she wouldn't have to face his reaction. Her foolish honesty had left her choking on her foot again.

Jack watched her retreat with mixed emotions. She had just set up a major road block. If he pushed her to act on the attraction, what would it do to her psyche? Her rigid façade masked a quiet sadness and an irresistible vulnerability.

By the time she returned with the hot dogs, she had erected a wall again. He let her hide. Until she trusted him, he wouldn't be able to reach her.

At least she enjoyed the football game. Her verbal outbursts at the referee gained her a legion of admirers among the hometown crowd. She had a detailed knowledge of the game, and he half-suspected she could have led the team better than the coach, Mr. Hurley.

"I'll bet you were a cheerleader in high school, with all the football players following you around," Jack said on the walk home.

"You'd lose that bet." She crossed her arms in front of her. "I was the bookworm in braces, and the only time the football players came near me was when I had to tutor one so he wouldn't get kicked off the team."

Her body trembled, but he wasn't sure if the cool air or the apparently painful memories were the cause.

"You should have told them to take a hike."

"You don't do that when your father is the coach."

"So *that's* the reason you know so much about football."

Leah didn't miss a step but her bright mood had taken a radical about-face. "I like football in spite of my father, not because of him. He never quite forgave me for being born . . . a girl."

"I'm sure he's proud of you now."

"Like you, I have a poor orphan status, but even before, I don't think he had any idea of what I did for a living."

That wasn't exactly true. Her father had been aware of how well she had done, but he had resented her for it. As a high school coach in a college town, he had dreamed of the big break that would catapult him to the upper ranks. A break that never came.

Through the years his bitterness grew. Every success that she achieved, he tried to destroy with cruel words and insinuations. Perhaps if she had seen that at the time instead of years later, she might have been a little easier on herself.

"We're here," Jack said.

Leah shook her head. Pushing her depressing thoughts to the back of her mind, she smiled. "Thanks for the game, but I really should head back to the city."

"I thought we were going to review those figures."

"By the time we get to the office it will be eleven o'clock. And you have your brother to consider."

"We can work from here."

She needed some space. He had managed to get more information out of her than her co-workers had gleaned in ten years. "We need the computer."

"I have one."

"With a modem?"

"Of course." Apparently, he wasn't going to let her out gracefully.

"I don't know. I should just call for a car."

"No way. If we don't work tonight, I can't write off the cost of that pretzel."

Despite her mixed emotions, she felt herself grinning. "All right. One hour." She refused to admit, even to herself, that Jack had anything to do with her decision. The work had to be done.

The study in Jack's house doubled as the guest room. He sat at the desk, leaving Leah with no where to work but on the bed. The intimate surroundings seemed to unsettle her. For the better part of an hour she sat Indian style as she tried to read through the pages of print-outs he had imported from the main computer.

He kept the conversation strictly to the reports, and slowly, she began to relax. She lay on her stomach with her knees bent and her chest propped up by two pillows.

Rock music blared through the halls. A sharp knock on the wall got Tim to lower the volume.

When the music stopped altogether, he glanced at his watch. One A.M. "I think we should pack it in."

Apparently, Leah had packed it in a while ago. Her arms, folded across a pile of reports, cradled her head. Eyes closed, she breathed the slow, steady rhythm of sleep. He didn't know whether to be flattered that she had finally relaxed around him, or insulted that she could so completely ignore him.

In sleep she lost the nervous tension that ruled every fiber of her existence. He eased the papers out from beneath her and covered her with a light blanket. Consideration had little to do with his decision to leave her sleeping; pure selfishness motivated him. If she stayed the night, he could spend another day with her.

Chapter Five

Leah buried her head under the blanket and tried to ignore the unfamiliar noise. *What was that infernal racket?* A car horn, a street fight, even the sirens of passing police cars were normal, but this annoying droning went on forever. She tossed the covers off and let out a startled gasp.

"Oh, great." She glanced around the pale blue room. Jack's jacket hung on a chair where he had left it the night before. The reports she had been studying sat casually on the desk as a glaring reminder that she had accomplished little more than making a fool of herself again.

She had to leave, but how? Unlike New York, where taxis run along every street, she had no idea how to get home. She was a prisoner of the suburbs!

Outside, a neighbor cut his front lawn and children played in the street. New Jersey seemed more than the geographical five miles away from New York City. It was another world. She slipped off the bed and straightened the covers.

She stepped into the hallway and headed for the kitchen. No one seemed to be up. With any luck she could find a phone book to call for a car. As she entered the kitchen, she saw Jack's little brother drinking milk straight from the container.

He turned and his mouth gaped, mirroring her own shock. Around his neck he wore a giant snake. She let out a yelp and backed into the wall.

"Oh, sorry," Tim muttered. "Poseidon won't hurt you."

She remained motionless until she realized that the animal posed no threat. The quick shot of adrenaline brought her fully awake. Finally, a mix of curiosity and fascination drew her closer. "You keep a snake as a pet?"

"A boa constrictor," he corrected, as if that made a huge difference. "They don't bite. Want to hold him?"

"No, thank you."

He removed Poseidon and held the snake out toward her. "Have you got something against reptiles?"

"Not really. I've dated a few in my time."

Tim's laughter reminded her of his older brother, and thoughts of Jack reminded her that she had spent the night in his house. She needed to return to the safety of her own apartment, hopefully before Jack could stop her.

She stroked her hand tentatively over the animal's surprisingly dry skin. "Are there any taxis around here?"

"I'll wake Jack."

"No!" She hadn't meant to sound so sharp, but she wasn't ready to face him.

How had she fallen asleep, in a strange house no less? She was used to working on little or no sleep. The fresh air of the suburbs must have shocked her system.

"You don't understand, Ms. Matthews. If I let you take a taxi home, my brother will make my life miserable. I get in enough trouble on my own—I don't need your help."

"Your brother's tough on you, huh?"

"That's putting it mildly. So you'll stay until he gets up?"

She couldn't believe she was allowing this teenager to emotionally blackmail her. Manipulating women must run in the family. "Is there a bakery around here? The least I can do is pick up some breakfast."

"There's one two blocks up. I'll go."

"No. These old bones need the exercise."

He arched one eyebrow in a suggestive manner more endearing than insulting. "You're not old."

"The same age as your brother."

Tim made a face of disbelief. "Can't be. He was born an old man."

Not the Jack she knew. She sighed and stepped out into the cool morning air. Perhaps she didn't know Jack at all. Their affair had ended before it began.

Jack stumbled into the living room. Hopefully, Mr. Nelson's early morning landscaping projects hadn't awakened Leah too. Apparently the man had a different internal clock than the rest of the civilized world.

"Putting in those late hours with the boss

must be exhausting," Tim joked of his disheveled appearance.

"Don't talk about her like that," Jack snapped. He sat down in the chair across from his brother. "And put that snake away before she wakes up and sees it."

"She saw Poseidon. Said he reminded her of a guy she used to date."

Jack ignored the dig, apparently meant for him. "She's up?"

Tim laughed. "Up and out before you, you sorry sack of . . ."

"Watch your language. And why didn't you wake me before she left?"

"Chill out. She just took a walk to the bakery to pick up some breakfast."

"And you let her?" She was probably half way back to New York by now. Or maybe not—she didn't know where or when the buses ran.

"Unlike me, she doesn't need your permission to go out by herself."

"How long ago?"

"Ten minutes or so." Tim glanced out the window. "She's on her way back now. Imagine that, she managed to walk two blocks without help from you."

"Is this 'National Pick On Your Brother'

day?" Jack rose and walked to the door. As Leah stepped inside, he relieved her of the grocery bag. "Good morning."

Her ponytail bobbed as she shook her head. "What's left of it."

"It's only eight-thirty. And *I* was up until one o'clock this morning working."

Leah glared at him. Obviously, she didn't want to be reminded that she had drifted off so soundly in his presence.

"Perhaps you need some coffee." He took the package into the kitchen. Did she think she was feeding an army? Besides the two bakery boxes, she had bought bacon, eggs, and waffles.

And a toothbrush. He chuckled as she yanked it from his hand.

"Don't you think a dozen donuts with all the other food is a bit excessive?" he asked.

"I didn't know what kind you liked, and I had to get three of each so there were no fights over the chocolate or the glazed.

"How diplomatic."

"It's called 'covering your rear end' and it's the first rule of marketing. Remember it."

"What, no sausage?"

She snapped her fingers and muttered, "Oh, shoot. I knew I forgot something."

Tim walked in the kitchen and grabbed two donuts. "Thanks for breakfast, Ms. Matthews. Gotta go. I've got practice today."

"Tim," she called after him. "Try turning your body to the right a bit more when you punt the ball. You'll get more distance."

"Your boss is a jock. She couldn't possibly be an ice queen," Tim noted cheerfully on his way out the door.

Jack noticed her flinch from the backhanded compliment. Although she was probably aware of her reputation among the men in the office, it still had to hurt. At work, she went out of her way to make her staff feel appreciated though she kept them at a distance. "I never said you were an ice queen."

"I'm sure he was quoting your good pal, Randy." She took a frying pan from the dish drainer. His first instinct was to duck but she merely handed it to him. "You'll have to cook breakfast. The kitchen is another room where I don't excel."

"Would you stop picking on yourself? You've got a brilliant mind."

She rolled her eyes and sighed. "Grand! It's nice to know you used me for my mind instead of my body."

"That's not true, Leah."

"I don't want to talk about it."

"Well, I do." He caught her arm as she tried to walk away. "You made an accusation. I should have the right to defend myself. I didn't spend time with you because I wanted to pump you for information."

Her eyes narrowed angrily. "Correct me if I'm wrong. We spent four days together and I can't seem to recall you mentioning you were interviewing with Rockford Industries."

Jack said nothing, convicting himself by his silence.

"I thought not." She took a doughnut from the box and nibbled on the edge.

"I needed the job," he finally said.

"Why didn't you tell me that from the beginning?"

"And you would have listened?"

"Yes."

"Boloney. You would have taken one look and said, *Ex-jock. He can't possibly have a brain.* I had eighteen interviews before I found this job. And in seventeen of those interviews do you know the first question I was asked?"

She shook her head.

"*Aren't you the Olympic runner?* They never even looked at my résumé. I don't want to be known for the rest of my life as a guy who made a career out of running around in spandex."

Despite her resentment, she felt the corners of her mouth lifting.

"You smiled," he noted with a grin of his own.

"I did not." He had smoothly detoured the focus of her anger. She was the injured party.

He raised a hand, hesitated, then brushed it against the tip of her nose. "Powdered sugar."

His closeness made her feel awkward. She took a step back to widen the distance between them, but it wasn't far enough to block out his masculine smell. Again, he had managed to throw her off-balance with little conscious effort.

He poured a cup of coffee and offered it to her. She wrapped her fingers around the mug of the strong, steaming brew and joined him at the kitchen table. A shot of caffeine should jolt her back into the world of the sane.

"I needed a job with regular hours and insurance benefits. The school wouldn't let Tim participate in interscholastic sports without it. I specifically didn't mention the interview because I didn't want you to think I had asked you out because you worked for Rockford. What happened between us wasn't planned."

She lowered her head. "All right. So maybe you had a good reason to hurt me, but it doesn't change the fact that I feel like the biggest fool in the world."

"I'm sorry."

"That makes me feel a whole lot better."

His hand covered hers. "I'm not apologizing for spending time with you. I wanted that and so did you."

Her routine denial remained unspoken. She pulled back her hand, but a tingling sensation remained. "Are you going to cook breakfast?"

"You're changing the subject."

"I thought we'd finished." Holding a post-mortem on the death of their brief relationship kept the pain alive. She wanted to forget. No matter what his excuse, he still hadn't been honest with her. He hurt her and she had made it so . . .

"Easy?" he asked.

"What?" she stammered. Had she spoken her thoughts aloud?

He held up an egg. "Sunny side up or over-easy?"

"Oh." She shrugged and let out a relieved sigh. "Whatever. While you're cooking, I need to call about a car."

"I'll drive you back."

"You don't have to."

"I said I would."

"Would it do me any good to argue?"

"Only delay the inevitable," he said. "Unless you prefer to spend the day here arguing about how you'll get home."

"You can't imagine how appealing that sounds, but I'll pass." She placed her hand over her heart in feigned disappointment. "I already have plans for this afternoon."

"I'll bet," he grumbled as he cracked the eggs into the frying pan.

Her temper flared. "Are you calling me a liar?"

"No. I only meant you would rather spend the day cleaning your apartment than being with me." He sounded so genuinely hurt that she bit her bottom lip to keep from grinning. She would not fall for that sorrowful glint in his eyes and the tempting pout on his lips.

"That depends. You are definitely more fun than cleaning the toilet, but you pale by comparison to the thrill and excitement of watching the freezer defrost."

To her surprise, he laughed. "I think I've been insulted."

"Are you insulted that I promised to visit my aunt, or that I like to watch the freezer defrost?"

He threw up his hands. "You win. I'll drive you back to the city after breakfast."

"Thank you." Even if she hadn't promised Aunt Mary a visit, spending more time with Jack wasn't wise. Her awareness of him never wavered. Without the distractions of work, she might not be able to keep her mind off him. The outcome was yet to be determined.

"Aren't you going to invite me in for a cup of coffee?," Jack asked as she reached for the handle of the Jeep.

"It's so difficult to park in the city," Leah said with a hint of feigned concern that didn't fool him. For the last ten minutes she sat perched in the front seat, readying herself for a quick escape.

"I'll find a spot—unless you don't want me to come up. Then just say so."

Backed into a corner, she shrugged. "It's

up to you, but it will have to be instant coffee. I'm already behind today."

"And heaven forbid you throw off your schedule," he gently teased. That she had taken time off to attend the football game last night still amazed him.

She smiled. "You've never met my aunt."

He parked the Jeep a few blocks from her building. Leah stopped in a small market for milk, then, at a quick pace common to most city dwellers, she led him to her brownstone.

She lived in one of the nicer areas of Manhattan, a few blocks off of Central Park. Once inside, she locked three dead bolts.

"I've been robbed twice," apparently she felt the need to explain.

"Why not move?"

"It's the same everywhere. And I've been here ten years. Rent control makes this more affordable than most places." At the door, she kicked off her sneakers and padded across the mauve carpet toward the kitchen. "Have a seat. I'll start the coffee."

Jack sank into the pillow back sofa. The sparsely furnished room of well crafted, Art Deco furniture gave the appearance of space in the small apartment. Pictures and plants reflected the subtle elegance of the owner.

On a *good* day, his house never looked this neat.

"Watch some television if you want. I have to take a quick shower."

Restlessly he paced the room, looking for some clue into the mind of his reluctant hostess. She displayed no photographs of friends or family. Her apartment seemed more like a show piece than a home. He glanced through the video library of old black and white classics. Where was the color in her life?

His gaze rested on the last video in the collection. *Instructional Belly Dancing*? The case was empty so he figured the cassette must be inside the VCR. Unable to resist, he hit the play button and stepped back to watch.

The step by step process of the Middle Eastern dance conjured up images of Leah in a harem costume doing the *Dance of the Seven Veils*.

The whistle of the tea kettle brought him back to earth. He stopped the tape, but not before Leah had entered the room.

She pushed her hand into the damp mass of ringlets forming around her face. Her cheeks turned as pink as the sweatshirt she wore. "What are you doing?"

"You told me to watch TV. I didn't know it was in there." Remembering her penchant for honesty, he sucked in a large gulp of air and said, "All right. I did know it was in there."

"I think you should leave." She pivoted around and sprinted to the kitchen.

Leah folded her arms on the counter. She never should have allowed him inside her apartment. He had invaded her last refuge. She had no place left to hide.

Footsteps came up behind her. "I'm sorry, Leah."

"I'm not blaming you. I just want you to go."

"No. You're blaming yourself, which is worse." He placed a hand on her shoulder. "I'm a slimy, sneaking snake. That's my fault, not yours."

"You're not slimy," she mumbled.

His laughter echoed through the room. "Holy cow! She made a joke!"

She reached back and smacked his hard chest. "Stop making fun of me."

"I'm not making fun of you." He leaned against the counter and ran his finger along the side of her flushed cheek. "I'm sure you're just studying it for the health benefits."

"It's actually very good aerobic exercise."

Jack nodded, but an amused glint in his eyes said he knew better.

Something had happened to her in Hawaii. She was changing. Although it scared her, she had no idea how to stop the process.

She gazed up at him and her heart skipped two beats. He had an invisible hold over her heart that all the anger, pain and denial couldn't sever. Keeping him at a distance became more difficult with each passing day.

"I better make that coffee," she said.

"Never mind." His hand cupped the side of her neck and held her still as he brushed a whisper of a kiss across her mouth. "I'll see you Monday."

He was gone before she had time to figure out what had happened. She stared at the closed door. Disappointment clouded her ability to think. Reflexively, she raised a finger to her lips. A warmth still lingered where his mouth had touched hers.

Why had he left so abruptly? She sighed with a combination of resignation and regret. He picked a strange time to be noble. She should appreciate his gesture, but all she knew was that she was alone again.

Jack stopped his Jeep in front of the building and glanced up at the second story apartment. He'd never known a woman of such beauty who was so completely unaware of her effect on the opposite sex.

He couldn't be with her and not think about what might have been if he'd been honest from the start. Leah seemed to need more time than he had patience. He would find a way to break through that granite wall of hers soon, or he would die trying.

Chapter Six

Leah pasted a bright smile on her face and walked into her aunt's living room. The furniture had survived ten years longer than Aunt Mary's thirty year marriage. It might have something to do with the plastic covers on the sofa and chairs—a torture in the summer because the frugal woman saw no point in wasting electricity on air conditioning.

The drapes remained closed until late afternoon to spare the upholstery from the effects of harsh sunlight. Leah always felt like she had walked into a tomb that had been sealed in the fifties.

Aunt Mary wore a frown of disapproval.

"Did you forget to pick up your dry cleaning, dear?"

Leah wiped her palms across the legs of her jeans, the first pair she had bought since college. "No. They're comfortable."

"For a youngster perhaps, but you're not a teenager any more." Aunt Mary's tailored black dress reminded Leah a little too much of her own wardrobe.

At nineteen, when she needed to present an image of maturity, the clothes had worked as her shield. Now, as a representative of the fashion industry, she should present a younger image.

She kissed her aunt and sat down in the chair. "How are you feeling?"

"I don't want to complain . . ."

But you will, Leah thought. That was the main reason her own daughter seldom visited. For the next half hour Aunt Mary carped on about her aches and pains. Leah nodded and smiled at the appropriate moments, but her thoughts dwelled on Jack and his tender kiss.

"Leah?" Mary's strident voice broke into her quiet memories.

"Yes?"

"I called your office yesterday and your

assistant said you had left. Do you think it's wise to leave early?"

Leah drew her brows together in thought. "I left at five o'clock."

Mary shrugged. "It's your career, but you wouldn't want the boss to think you're slacking off."

"That's not a problem. Besides, I'm thinking about making a move to another company."

"Oh, Leah, don't be foolish. You won't find another position like yours."

"Thank you." Most of the time Leah attributed her aunt's warnings to her reserved British upbringing. Today, she couldn't help but feel the sting of an insult.

Her family seemed to think her success was a fluke. Her father had been more direct: he had asked if she'd had an affair with her boss. Ironically, the only person who understood and admired her abilities was Jack.

"I *have* had other offers," Leah reminded her.

"But nothing in writing. You're almost thirty. You don't have much time left."

Leah groaned silently. *Here it comes. The find-yourself-a-husband speech.* She knew it by heart. According to her aunt, her biological clock was tick, tick, ticking away. Leah wasn't up to the lecture today. "I can't stay. I have a few errands to take care of."

Aunt Mary expelled a long, suffering sigh. "Don't worry about me, dear. I'm sure I'll get by."

Leah left with a shroud of guilt that surprisingly lifted the moment she reached the street. She wasn't sure if her family's lack of confidence had made her feel so insecure, or vice versa. All she knew was that nothing would change unless she broke the cycle of self-doubt.

"Wait, Jim . . . yes, I know we decided . . . I'm sure it was just a misunderstanding . . . yes, I'll talk to Ellen right away and get back to you." Leah slammed the receiver down with a resounding crash. She was tired of running interference with the sales people.

Sue jumped at the uncharacteristic display of anger. "Something wrong, Ms. Matthews?"

"What could be wrong? Jim is in a meeting with one of our biggest retailers, looking like a complete idiot because Ms. Rockford promised a delivery date three weeks before we even begin manufacturing the line. Not to even mention the six week lead time for the accessories from Asia."

"You'll arrange something. You always do."

Yes, she always did, and she never said a word about Ellen's mistakes. Not this time. If Ellen wanted to play the part of president, then she could darn well take responsibility for her mistakes.

"Call and see if she's free," Leah said. She ran through the raw materials inventory to see if it was feasible even to try to honor the promise. The schedule could be rearranged, but the cost in overtime and air freight would cut the profit margin considerably.

"She said she's got a minute," Sue called out.

A minute? As if a minute would be sufficient to straighten out the mess Ellen had made. Leah stormed out of her office and down the hall.

Ellen sat behind the desk of her corner office, admiring her manicure, as Leah walked in and shut the door. "It will have to be quick, Leah. I have a hair appointment with Raphael and he's such a bear if I'm late."

"I wouldn't want you to leave Raphael

hanging," Leah sniped, and slipped into a chair.

Oblivious to the sarcasm, Ellen smiled. "I notice you've been a bit more daring with your wardrobe lately. Is there a special man in your life?"

Leah tugged at the hem of her knee-length dress. Although red was not her favorite color, the vibrant shade lived up to its reputation for making a person feel more aggressive. "My love life is not the problem. Your promise to Richard Robbins is."

Her boss shrugged. "What's wrong? I told him he could have the first run off the line to get a jump on the competition. He *is* our biggest buyer."

"You told him he could have it before we are even due to start cutting. It can't be done."

"Have them start earlier."

"Just like that?" The woman had no idea what was involved in manufacturing a line of clothing. How had she grown up in Edward Rockford's house, yet learned so little about the business that had paid for her fancy socialite life? "Even if we could get it finished, the cost overruns would have us just breaking even."

"I don't care. I will not let Mercury Sportswear beat us to the punch on this one. Marcus will have his line ready by then."

Ah, Leah thought. *This had nothing to due with business.* Ellen's juvenile rivalry with her ex-husband would cost the managing directors their annual bonus—not to mention the company's reputation if they couldn't meet their new obligation.

"Marcus doesn't have nearly the customer base we do, and his line is smaller."

"I'm not going to argue on this one. I'm the president . . ."

"You want to run this company?" Leah's voice pitched as she came to her feet. "Go ahead. You meet with buyers, you deal with the advertising people, and you tell me how you want to market each line. I won't do anything unless I receive a direct order from you."

The unexpected outburst left Ellen momentarily speechless. She stammered several times but couldn't come up with a coherent word.

Leah tapped her heel impatiently against the floor. "Well?"

"Calm down," Ellen finally managed, in a

patronizing tone. "I didn't mean to step on your toes."

"You didn't step, you stomped. If you have a problem with the way I'm doing my job, then replace me. If not, then check with me before making promises that leave the rest of us looking like fools."

Ellen reclined in her chair and clapped her hands together. "So, the little kitten has finally sharpened her claws. You never stood up to my father like that."

"If that's supposed to be an apology, save it. We'll get the line out in time, but only because our reputation is at stake."

"I knew you would." Ellen cocked an eyebrow dangerously. "And Leah. Don't forget whose name is on the company. My deluded father may have thought the sun rose and set with you, but no one is irreplaceable."

Leah paused at the door and turned back. The veiled threat had no effect. "I know. But no job is irreplaceable either."

She returned to her office on an adrenaline rush. It felt great to get that off her chest. She relieved more stress this morning than she had at her dance class the evening before. Her only regret was that she hadn't said something long ago.

"Is it safe to come in?" Jack asked from the doorway.

She folded her hands behind her head, and relaxed in the plush leather chair. "Why wouldn't it be?"

"Sue said you were in with the boss. That's never a pleasant affair."

Her enigmatic smile revealed nothing. "What can I do for you?"

Since Saturday she had kept him at a distance. Not that he expected anything less in the office, but a slight acknowledgment of his existence in the elevator wouldn't send the rumor mill into overtime.

"I have the revised production schedule ready for your approval."

She took the papers he offered, but placed them face down on the desk. "Thanks, but there's a slight problem."

He frowned. "Aren't you going to look at it first?"

"I don't have to. I'm sure it is perfect based on the information you were given."

Jack bit back an angry retort. He thought he had worked his way beyond the deliberate attempts to undermine him. Although Leah never commented on a mistake due to misinformation, he felt as if he lost credibility in her eyes. "All right. What's wrong?"

"Would you care to sit down?"

He nodded and sat in the chair across from her.

"Do you mind taking a trip down to the plant in South Carolina, to see if Bob Jamison can push production forward by six weeks?"

"Why not call him?"

"After all the work the two of you put into this already, I don't think it's something that should be done over the phone. If *I* demand the change, I'm a pushy broad. If you do it, you're an assertive man. They're a bit chauvinistic down there."

"What happened?"

"Mercury Sportswear will have their spring collection ready by then, and Ellen wants ours in the stores at the same time. Can you do it?"

He bristled at the implication. "I'll handle it."

"Don't get defensive. If I thought you couldn't, I'd go myself." Her smile broke the tension. "I thought you might have a problem leaving Tim alone overnight."

The woman could throw a curve faster

than a major league pitcher. One minute she was pure business and then, without warning, she was concerned about his family commitments. "Tim can stay with our aunt."

"Then I suggest you make some calls and set up a meeting with Bob. Take him to dinner someplace nice with his wife. I'll have a corporate card issued before you leave. For now, ask Sue to make the plane and hotel reservations on my charge account."

"I'd rather do it myself."

She nodded and handed him her charge card. "Are they still giving you a hard time?"

He tilted his head to the side. "Would you care if they were?"

"Yes," she answered with surprising sincerity. "You're kind of like a new kitchen gadget—I didn't think I needed you but now, unfortunately, I can't seem to work without you."

"Thank you . . . I think." He rose and walked to the door, shaking his head. "Although I'm not sure I like being compared to a food processor."

Her green eyes sparkled with the hint of amusement. "You wanted to make an impression on me."

That wasn't the impression he had in

mind. However, their relationship did appear to be taking a turn for the better. Her tone was light, almost flirtatious. She seemed more relaxed—a good sign that things were improving.

"Wipe that grin off your face, Jack. You're not out of the dog house yet."

"At least I'm not on a leash any more."

As he left the office he heard her soft laughter. Before his ego took on a life of its own, he reminded himself that she might just be laughing because she wouldn't have to see him for the next few days.

Leah poked her hand out from under the covers and shut off the annoying alarm clock. *It's just another day,* she tried to convince herself. That it was also the first anniversary of her twenty-ninth birthday had nothing to do with her lousy mood.

Swinging her feet off the side of the bed, she rose and stumbled to the bathroom. On automatic pilot, she turned on the shower. As she reached for her toothbrush, she caught a glimpse of herself in the mirror. Like a neon sign flashing, *You're getting old*, one gray hair spiraled out from her mass of curls.

"That's it," she groaned and pulled the offending hair from her head. The sharp pain faded in a second, but she used it as an excuse to grant herself a sick day—her first at Rockford Industries.

Once she had made all her calls into the office, she decided to spend the crisp autumn day pampering herself. Alone she didn't have nearly the fun she had hoped she would. By two o'clock in the afternoon, boredom overcame her. She headed home, with nothing to look forward to over the long Columbus Day weekend but more of the same.

As much as she hated to admit it, she missed Jack. She superimposed his face on every man that passed on the crowded city streets. Her grasp on reality was slipping.

"Get a grip," she muttered to herself. She had survived twenty-nine years without him.

Her thirtieth birthday bothered her more than she had expected. On the bright side, according to the experts, she was reaching her prime. She moaned. Some bright side, when the only thing to go home to was a box of chocolate cookies and an old movie about lost love.

The doorbell woke Leah from a sound sleep. She glanced at her watch. Only seven o'clock? The movie had finished and a television screen of white snow hissed at her. She hit the pause button before shuffling across the carpet to answer the door. Through the peek hole she saw a striking array of brightly colored balloons. Either a circus had camped out in her building, or her cousin had a strange sense of humor.

She pulled the door open.

"Happy birthday," Jack's voice rang out from behind the helium filled bouquet.

"Go away," she grumbled. She couldn't have looked worse if she tried. Dressed in her old flannel nightgown and white sweat socks, she presented the picture of middle-aged frump.

Jack, by comparison, looked the very model of male perfection, from the soles of his leather shoes to the collar of his white shirt. "I can see you were expecting me," he noted with a laugh. "That's quite a fetching outfit."

He maneuvered his way into the apartment and let the bouquet fly up to the ceiling. Other than his light joke, he didn't seem put off by her appearance.

She slouched down in the sofa with a deep sigh. "What are you doing here?"

His smile had her heart doing flip-flops. "You didn't think I'd let your birthday pass without acknowledging it, did you?"

"Of course not. You've been waiting to take your revenge on me. You probably caught an early flight back just to make sure you made it in time to torment me."

"Wrong. I caught an early flight so that I could take you out for your birthday."

She raised her arms to emphasize her less than charming appearance. "It is usually customary to *ask* a lady first, so she can prepare."

He slipped his hands into his pockets and shrugged. "You would have said no—and *don't* deny it. Now, get changed or I'll take you out dressed like that." Seeing the stubborn determination in his stance, she didn't argue.

She *did* need to get out for a while. For most of the day she had been miserable about her thirtieth birthday. After only five minutes in his company, her spirits had risen like a phoenix from the ashes of despair—not that she would admit that to Jack.

"All right." She sprang to her feet with renewed enthusiasm. "You can tell me how it went at the plant. It will be a business dinner."

He blocked her path as she tried to pass. "No. I'm taking you out on a date. I'm paying. And if you're a good girl, you might even get a kiss at the end of the night."

"Then I'll have to be a bad girl."

His mouth lifted in a blatantly seductive grin. "I can only hope."

She let out a frustrated yelp and scooted around him. His laughter followed her as she made her way through the maze of red ribbons dangling from the balloons. At the bedroom door she paused and turned back. "By the way, where are we going?"

"You're the birthday girl. Wherever you want."

She closed her eyes and exhaled slowly. Her preference would be to skip dinner altogether and spend the evening at home with Jack. Not a very professional attitude for a boss toward her subordinate, but the truth all the same.

"I'll be ready in a few minutes."

She changed into a pale peach dress, adorned with tiny pearl buttons down the front and along the wide cuffs. A quick glance in the mirror boosted her confidence.

In this dress, she didn't look a day over twenty-nine. After applying light blush and lip gloss, she returned to the living room.

Jack turned and stared for what seemed an eternity. His expression unreadable, she automatically assumed the worst.

"You don't like the dress?" she asked. "I can change."

Shaking his head, he took a step closer. "You look beautiful." Her uncertainty melted beneath the intensity of his gaze. Her head and her heart were caught in a tug-of-war, and she felt as if she was being pulled in opposing directions.

Tonight, she didn't want to deal with reality. She was going to live the fantasy. At midnight, her Cinderella dream would end, but for now, she wanted the glass slipper. She caught his hand in hers. If she didn't go now, she might lose her nerve.

Chapter Seven

Leah leaned against the wall outside her apartment and sighed. The evening couldn't have been more perfect if she had planned it herself: dinner at a French restaurant, and a movie that could only be called a woman's film. Jack had even stayed awake, something the few other men in the theater hadn't managed to accomplish.

How could she have been so dumb to agree to this? Did she think she would be any less susceptible to his charm, now than she had been in Hawaii?

"Thank you." She rose on tip-toes to place a kiss on his cheek.

He turned his head to meet her lips. Apparently a chaste peck on the cheek wasn't what he had in mind. She was swept into his embrace, held against him by a pair of powerful arms. He kissed her tenderly, sweetly drawing a response she could no more control than conceal. Warning bells rang in her conscience but she ignored them. All caution was pushed from her mind. To her embarrassment, he was the first to pull back.

He lifted his mouth from hers and drew a breath. "We're making a scene in the hall."

"I guess I was a good girl," she muttered. She inserted the key in the lock and pushed the door open. "Well, it's late. You probably have to be heading back now."

"I can stay a while."

"Tim?"

"He's having a great time with his aunt and his cousins."

"Oh." Part of her wanted to prolong the evening, but she knew she would only end up deeper in trouble. She had too many feelings for Jack to be just a friend, and too much invested in her career to indulge in an office romance. Dare she hope that he too would realize they had made a mistake by going out tonight?

"Aren't you going to offer me a cup of your famous instant coffee?" he asked.

What harm could a simple cup of coffee do? She showed him to the living room and disappeared into the kitchen. Moments later she returned with a tray. Jack had made himself comfortable on the sofa. She took the seat next to him.

"What do you say we take a ride down to the shore tomorrow? It's beautiful this time of year, and we have a long weekend."

She shook her head. "I have plans already."

"Then Sunday."

"I don't think this is a good idea."

"You don't like the ocean? How about the mountains?"

His eagerness to please made her decision that much more difficult. Office romances never worked—especially between a supervisor and a subordinate. "I'm not talking about the location. I'm talk about going out again."

"You didn't enjoy yourself tonight?"

Leah expelled a heavy sigh. He wasn't going to make this easy on her. "Tonight was very special. But that doesn't mean we should let it happen again."

He cocked his eyebrow. "And why is that?"

"For one thing, I'm your boss."

"I'm aware of that. And I don't have a problem with it. Our working relationship has nothing to do with our personal relationship."

Perhaps not to him, but she couldn't separate the two. How could she deal with him objectively when her feelings were so subjective?

"What's really bothering you, Leah?"

A loaded question if ever she heard one. After all her sermons to her staff about the inappropriateness of office romances, she felt like a hypocrite. She didn't think for a second that Jack would use their relationship to further his career, but she didn't know if she could treat him fairly because of it.

Sitting so close, he posed an overpowering distraction. She sprung to her feet to put distance between them. "Why does this have to be so complicated?"

"It doesn't. You're making it a problem. What we do outside of work is nobody's business."

If only that were true. She thought of Ellen's numerous affairs with the men who worked for her. That kind of reputation Leah could gladly do without. She didn't want what she and Jack shared to become an office joke.

She leaned against the wall and stared down at the parquet tile. "I'm thinking about *you*."

He groaned at her feeble excuse. "You are not—you're covering your own rear end. I believe you once told me that's the first rule of marketing."

"Maybe I am," she conceded. "I fought very hard to build the reputation I have."

He came to his feet and stood directly in front of her. Hurt and anger shone in the depths of his cobalt-blue eyes. "And a relationship with me would sully your precious reputation?"

"Not you. Anyone."

"That's ridiculous." He dismissed her point with a wave of his hand. "Just because you're an executive doesn't mean you can't be a woman too."

She pushed her fingers into the mass of curls falling in her face. "You don't understand."

"Let me ask you something, Leah."

She lifted a wary gaze in his direction. "What?"

"Would it make a difference to you if I was *your* boss?"

Her expression reflected her confusion and sorrow. She deliberated long and hard before answering. "Probably."

He shook his head. "Then I can't help you. I can't change this situation. You'll have to deal with this by yourself." Leaning forward, he pressed a kiss against her cheek. "When you've figured things out, you know where to find me."

"I can't change who I am, Jack."

"If that were true, you never would have gone out with me tonight. What you hate is that you can't control these changes."

She started to speak, but the protest died on her lips. Folding her arms across her chest, she huddled against the wall.

He knew she was hurting. He could see the emptiness in her shimmering eyes. Perhaps that was what she needed. If being without him hurt enough, she might choose the logical solution.

Leah leaned against the rail and looked down the deep center of the circular glass building. Every clothing manufacturer was represented on twenty floors of showrooms. Three days of intense meetings had left her little time to dwell on her broken heart—a heart she alone was responsible for breaking.

The trip to the Atlanta Fashion Mart had been a godsend. Not that she generally enjoyed unexpected problems, but the last minute jaunt had spared her from having to face Jack at work. A temporary reprieve, she knew.

Why couldn't she get beyond the fact that she was his boss? One monogamous relationship with a man she loved didn't put her in the same category as her indiscriminate boss. Who, besides her, even cared anymore? According to statistics, a high percentage of couples met their partners in the workplace.

Dozens of nagging questions, but the same answer always came back to her: she cared. Why? Just because she always assumed the man would have the better paying job didn't make it the golden rule. She had been known to be wrong. After all, until she met Jack, she had believed love was highly overrated.

"Leah?"

The voice calling to her over the groups of sellers and buyers sounded vaguely familiar. She turned and scanned the hall. The face of an old and dear friend greeted her warmly. "Marcus."

His grin widened. "I almost didn't recognize you. You've really blossomed. You must have a new man in your life."

She laughed. Despite the fact that he was right, she said, "How typically male to assume a woman can only blossom if a man is in her life."

"That's the law of nature, honey."

At forty-five, Marcus Chatsworth was still a striking man. Ellen didn't know what a gem she had lost. After Edward Rockford, Marcus had been one of the biggest influences in her professional life. He knew the business, a fact clearly reflected in the swift rise of Mercury Sportswear.

"What brings you here?" he asked.

"Business."

Her vague and guarded answer caused him to grin. "Don't worry. I'm not trying to trick you out of any company secrets."

She smiled. "You wouldn't get any."

"Still loyal to Ellen, I see," he noted admirably.

"To Edward's memory," she corrected.

Marcus knew there was no love lost between her and Ellen. They had spent many long evenings working together while his ex-wife carried on. Leah admired the fact that Marcus had stayed with Ellen as long as he had.

"I still have my spies around, and the word is, you should have been moved up to vice-president long ago. You're doing all the work anyway. She's holding you down, because you're letting her. It's time you moved on, kid."

"I've been thinking about it lately."

He paused as if trying to gauge the seriousness of her statement. "When you really mean that, come talk to me."

"Put it in writing and we'll talk, Marcus."

A spark of interest flashed in his eyes. "Wouldn't that just frost Ellen's cake, if you defected to the enemy camp? She's been jealous of you since the day Edward hired you." He looked at his watch and frowned. "I have an important meeting in ten minutes. I don't suppose you'll be at the Gabriel Charity Benefit tomorrow night?"

"You know I never go to those things. That's Ellen's domain. Besides, I'm going to be here a few more days."

He glanced toward a group of men and

women waving him over. "We'll talk again, soon." He popped a fatherly kiss on her cheek. "You look great. I really want to meet *him* someday."

After Marcus disappeared, she strolled through the mart checking out the competition. She wondered how serious Marcus had been. Would he, in fact, contact her again? Would she leave Rockford if he made her a decent offer?

The answer was an unequivocal yes. She needed a change in her life. A change she could control, she amended, remembering Jack's parting words to her.

Leaving Rockford would end her problems in that respect. If she were no longer his boss . . . if they didn't work together . . .

Leah shook her head and sighed. She had to come to some kind of resolution herself, not wait for fate or some outside force to make the decision for her.

Jack inhaled a breath of fresh air before entering the corner office. An odor reminiscent of a perfume shop assaulted him. Ellen pointed one blood-red fingernail toward the empty chair. "Have a seat."

He followed her directive. "You wanted to see me?"

"Yes. Are you familiar with the Gabriel Benefit?"

"It's a charity fund raiser put on by the fashion industry."

She pushed back a strand of hair from her face. "I thought Leah would be back in time, but it seems she'll be in Atlanta a few more days. Is it possible that you could attend in her place?"

If Leah had made the request herself he wouldn't have hesitated, but nothing had been mentioned before today. Her trip to Atlanta had come up at the last minute, in part, he suspected, to avoid him.

"Many of our biggest clients attend," Ellen went on to explain. "It's a great networking opportunity. You'd be doing Leah a big favor."

Phrased like that, he didn't have much of a choice. "I guess so. What time?"

"I'll have a car sent for you at seven."

"I'd rather drive myself."

Ellen nodded. "Whatever you decide."

Her agreement eased some of his lingering apprehension. In no way did he want this to be seen as anything more than a business dinner.

Fifteen minutes after he arrived at the black tie affair, Jack realized he had made a tactical error. Ellen, dressed to impress in red sequins, monopolized his attention from the moment she spotted him. If he tried to engage others in conversation she immediately cut in and moved him to the next group of people she wanted to impress.

He seethed, but held his tongue. Now he knew how a paid escort felt. In the presence of other women, her hand remained possessively on his arm, implying a relationship that didn't exist.

"There's someone you just *have* to meet," Ellen said with a malicious grin on her face. "Marcus. How are you?"

"Ellen," the older man said. With a cold nod of his head, he glanced toward Jack, disdain narrowing his dark eyes. "Picking them younger each year you get older."

"You sound jealous, darling. Jackson is my new marketing manager."

Jack noted the *my* in her comment, as if she owned him. His body went rigid, but Ellen didn't seem to notice.

"Leah failed to mention she was leaving

when I ran into her yesterday." Marcus grinned. "Now I'll make sure I get back to her on a position in my company."

"I bet you'd love that," she sneered. "Heaven knows you admired her like a besotted old fool for years."

"Careful, dear. Now *you* sound jealous."

"Don't flatter yourself. And Leah is not leaving," Ellen assured him, her eyes shooting daggers of resentment toward the older man. "Jack works under Leah."

Marcus' lip curled back in a sneer. "I thought they all work under you, dear. At least until you get bored with them."

Ellen tossed back her head and let out a piercing laugh that drew attention to them.

Jack lowered his head in embarrassment. So far he'd been paraded around like a trained bear, insulted by an ex-husband and generally judged as a gigolo by half the people in the place. And dinner hadn't even been served yet.

"Ms. Rockford. I have to be leaving."

"Don't tell me Marcus has upset you." Ellen tightened her fingers around Jack's arm. "He's been bitter ever since I kicked him out."

"Ellen, let the boy leave. He'll think

you're desperate. And desperation doesn't suit you any more than red sequins."

The ship was sinking, and fast. If he didn't bail out soon he would drown in a stormy sea. These two were so perfectly suited, Jack marveled that they bothered to divorce. They enjoyed the verbal sniping the way most couples enjoyed courting.

"I have family commitments waiting at home," Jack said, and removed her arm from his.

"A wife?" Marcus asked snidely. "Not that something like that would bother my ex-wife."

"Excuse me." Jack turned and disappeared into the crowd before he did something he might regret.

He should have followed his instincts. *You'd be doing Leah a big favor.* He could no more picture Leah at one of these affairs than at a Shriners' Convention. The only business conducted here was the kind Ellen Rockford had in mind. The kind that Leah despised.

He needed to speak with her before she heard about the evening from someone else. Regardless of her declaration that he should get out more, he had no interest in seeing other women. Nor did he want her to think he had.

Leah dropped her suitcases off at the apartment and went straight to the office. Most of the staff had left for the evening. Sue, coat and purse in hand, stopped as Leah entered.

"Ms. Matthews."

"You've been with me five years, Sue. I think you can call me Leah now." She smiled and shrugged out of her jacket.

While in Atlanta she had done a lot of thinking. Her stuffy, uptight attitude was in need of an adjustment. She had gained nothing by keeping her co-workers at a distance. When she watched the other women huddled together, exchanging amusing stories of parents, children and men, she felt left out. She wanted a taste of the female camaraderie she had missed most of her life.

No one would let her in until she made the first move. If she could learn to lighten up, they might accept her as a friend.

"So, did I miss anything while I was away?" she asked.

"I guess that depends on whether you want the grapevine news or you want to wait until a statement is issued in a company memo."

Sue's cryptic comments piqued her curiosity. "That's all right. Give me the dirt."

"The Black Widow has changed mates again. It's funny—I was just starting to think that I might have been wrong about him."

"Wrong about who?" Leah felt an uneasy twisting in the pit of her stomach.

"Jackson Brandt. According to Megan in accounting, Ellen canceled her date with Mike Walsh to take our Mr. Brandt to the Gabriel Benefit."

With Herculean strength, Leah kept the smile plastered on her face. "Well, it's really none of our business what they do after-hours."

She shouldn't be surprised, but somehow she was. Although she tended to ignore office gossip, most rumors were based in truth. There might be a perfectly logical explanation why Jack went with Ellen, although, try as she did, none came to mind.

The seasoned businesswoman rested her arms ontop of her desk and presented a brave show of indifference. Inside, the gawky little kid in braces felt one more rejection tear at her heart. Apparently four days had been too long to make a major decision about her relationship with Jack.

After checking through her messages and finding nothing pressing, she collected her purse and dance clothes from the closet. A strenuous workout would relieve some of the tension. And if she believed that, someone could sell her a vacation time-share in the swamps.

"I'll see you tomorrow, Sue." She was almost out the door when she ran into Jack.

He placed his hand on her arm to halt her exit. "Leah. Can I talk to you for a minute?"

She glared at him and removed his hand. "I'm late. I have a class." Sue's presence was a relief and an embarrassment. A relief because Jack wouldn't force the issue in front of her assistant, and an embarrassment because she had no logical excuse for her anger.

"It won't take much time."

"Have Sue make an appointment for tomorrow. I really have to leave." She slipped past him and sprinted for the elevator.

Jack watched her retreat. He expected initial resistance, but her attitude was much more. Her eyes only turned that shade of deep green when she was blazing mad. She had only been in the office ten minutes—surely word didn't travel that fast.

He turned toward Sue. Her frown of distaste answered his question before her words. "Did you want that appointment? Or perhaps Ms. Rockford can take care of what you need."

"Bad news travels fast in this place," he snapped.

"I wouldn't know what you mean." Sue slammed her desk drawer and stormed out of the office.

"You're not having much luck with the girls today, pal."

Out of the corner of his eye, Jack caught Randy's smirk. "How long have you been there?"

"Long enough. I see you decided to take my advice."

"What are you talking about?" Jack demanded.

"Ellen. It must have been some date. She never made it in today."

Jack pushed his hands in his pockets and

balled his fingers into tight fists. "Is that what you think?"

Randy raised his shoulders casually. "Hey, I'm not judging you. I say go for it."

"And I say, not on your life. When I realized it wasn't a business dinner I was out of there. The last I saw, Ellen was exchanging pleasantries with her ex-husband."

"You walked out on her? Are you out of your mind?" Randy's jaw sagged.

"I couldn't walk out on her since it wasn't a date. If she thought there was something more, that's her problem."

Obviously, it was his problem too. If the rumors flying around had reached Leah faster than the speed of light, by now the rest of the office believed the matter to be fact,—an unsettling thought in light of Ellen Rockford's history.

What could he do? Send a memo to all the department heads? Who would believe him? One thing was certain: he had to talk to Leah before her doubts about him made her retreat beyond reach.

Leah climbed the stairs to the second floor apartment with her usual weariness, her linen suit draped over one arm and a can of mace clutched tightly in her hand. Madam Justine's class had been brutal coming on top of an exhausting week. Her muscles hurt, her heart ached and her confidence had taken the express elevator to the basement.

What else could possibly go wrong today? She stepped into the hall. A chill ran along her spine. She was not alone. Pivoting quickly, she readied her trusty mace.

"Leah?"

Relief replaced fear as Jack stepped out of the shadows. An adrenaline rush sent goose bumps along her arm. "You scared the heck out of me."

"Sorry." His voice was clipped.

"What are you doing here?"

"I told you—I need to talk to you."

She searched her purse for her keys. "It couldn't wait?"

"Apparently not. Can we go inside?"

With an indifferent shrug, she opened the door and allowed him to pass in front of her.

The balloons he had given her last week had settled across the floor. Her suitcase was on the coffee table where she had dropped it in her haste to see Jack before he left the office. What a difference a few hours could make.

She hung her suit in the closet while Jack made himself a bit too comfortable in her apartment. An irrational resentment flared. She sat in the chair across from him and twirled her fingers in her lap. "Well, this is your tea party. What's on your mind?"

"Last evening."

She feigned consternation. "Last evening . . . let me see . . . it was a balmy Georgia night. The moon was full and I watched the World Series from my hotel room."

"That's not what I meant, and you know it."

"Sorry. Could you be more specific? Did you want to discuss world events, the President's new budget plan, or daily horoscopes?"

He frowned. "Can you be serious?"

"Yes, let's do be serious. It's so important for you to be taken seriously."

"Yes, it is."

Then why did you spend the evening with Ellen Rockford? she wanted to scream. Jealousy seared her like fire. "It's late. Make your point."

"I'm sure you've heard that I went to the Gabriel Benefit."

"Yes, I heard. Did you enjoy yourself?"

"No, I didn't."

"Too bad." She injected a note of sympathy to her voice. "Didn't care for the food?"

He clenched and unclenched his fingers. "I wouldn't know. I left before dinner."

"It's really none of my business what you do and with whom."

His face hardened to a stone mask. "What is it you think I did and with whom?"

"I try not to think about it." She tried, but unfortunately the nagging suspicion wouldn't leave her alone.

"You think I had an affair with Ellen," he snapped out with a controlled rage. She shook her head in denial, but he didn't seem to notice. "For the record, I went to that dinner because I was told that I was filling in for you. When I realized Ellen had her own agenda, I left. Alone."

She knew she was being completely irrational. In her heart she didn't believe he'd add himself to Ellen's collection, but the fact that he went at all smacked of betrayal. He should have refused the invitation no matter what the Black Widow told him. "Everyone thinks you did."

"I don't care what everyone else thinks. I only care what you think."

"I know you don't care about her." She stared at her trembling fingers, unnerved by the intensity of his blue eyes studying her.

He sprung to his feet and paced around the room. "I guess I should be thankful for that at least."

"Why?"

"Why? Why?" he shouted. "Are you blind, or just dense when it comes to me?"

"I must be," she muttered.

"For goodness sake—I'm in love with you!"

Profound shock rendered her speechless. She struggled for the air that had been sucked from her body.

"It's obvious that you don't want to deal with my feelings for you. I'm sorry if I've made you uncomfortable." He headed toward the door, paused and turned toward her. "No, I'm not sorry. I hope you're very uncomfortable."

He left the apartment with a slam of the door that rattled the walls. No more than he had rattled her emotions. *In love with her?* Why had he gone and said something like that?

Leah drew up her knees and wrapped her arms around them. In her entire life, no one had ever claimed to love her.

Chapter Eight

Through the bus window, Leah watched life pass by at sixty miles an hour. The view of the Palisades from the George Washington Bridge eased her apprehension, but only for a moment. Once the bus turned off the highway, she nervously scanned the street for a familiar landmark.

Instead of being so stubborn, she should have called for a car. She had to prove to herself that she could find her way. Jack made the commute every day. So what if he knew the route? After today, she would too.

Anxiety brought her back to reality. She was assuming too much. Maybe he didn't want to see her. He had managed to avoid her all week. Though she had been in and out of meetings . . . maybe it was her imagination.

Face it, Leah. He's ticked off big time and he has every reason to be. What she knew about love could fill a thimble—with room to spare.

She spotted a familiar bakery and pulled the cord for the driver to stop. The bus came to a halt at the corner. She descended the stairs and breathed a gulp of crisp air.

Packs of teenagers roamed the main street, most sporting high school sweatshirts and jackets. Her courage faded. Friday night was football night for the hometown Cougars. She didn't want her confrontation to take place in front of hundreds of spectators. Gathering the last remaining shreds of her pride, she tagged behind a group of cheering students to the campus field.

Once inside, she scanned the bleachers, looking for Jack. With her luck, he had decided not to attend tonight. A thunderous applause greeted the team as they came onto the field. Spotting Tim was easier than finding his brother.

Slowly, as if he wasn't quite sure who she

was, Tim approached the fence. He removed his helmet. "Hello Ms. Matthews."

"Leah," she corrected with a smile.

He glanced over her shoulder. "Where's Jack?"

She had been hoping Tim could tell her. "I'm not sure."

"He didn't say you'd be here." Tim shrugged ruefully and sent her a conspiratorial wink. "Lately he hasn't said much of anything. Least nothing I could repeat in front of a girl."

Leah felt her cheeks flush. Great! Jack was in a foul mood. Maybe showing up here wasn't one of her more brilliant ideas.

"He'll be here," Tim said. "He's driving me home."

"Hey, lover boy," the coach yelled out. "Is the game interfering with your social life?"

"I gotta go," Tim muttered shyly. He waved and sprinted back to his team.

Leah found a seat in the bleachers and awaited the opening kick-off. By the end of the first quarter she gave up looking for Jack. If he had planned to come, he would have arrived by now.

* * *

Jack ripped the keys from the Jeep and jogged through the parking lot. The high school marching band was putting on the half time show as he passed through the gate.

After the way he had ignored Tim the last few days, Jack wanted to be here for support. It wasn't Tim's fault that his love life was in shambles. He made his way over to the fence and waved his brother over.

"I'm sorry I'm late," Jack said.

"Where's Leah?"

Jack cocked an eyebrow. "What makes you think she's here? And who said you could call her Leah?" Obviously Tim had developed a bit of a crush on his boss. It must run in the family.

Tim puffed up his chest and stared down his nose. "*She* told me to call her Leah."

"And when was that, wise guy?"

" 'Bout an hour ago."

"She's here?" Jack ran a sweeping gaze through the crowded bleachers.

Tim shrugged. "She was. I haven't seen her since the kick-off. Is there something going on between the two of you?"

"I'm not sure. Do me a favor—go home with Aunt Ruth tonight."

Jack continued his visual search. She had

come on her own? That was a step in the right direction, but how far was she willing to go? Things would have to change between them.

The aroma of roasting chestnuts and frankfurters lingered on the breeze. Half time and hot pretzels. He knew where to find her.

He saw her, leaning against the side of the snack bar, deep in thought. Errant strands escaped from her loose ponytail, framing her face in a halo of golden brown curls. Dressed in her soft denim jeans and college sweatshirt, Leah looked more like a coed than a business executive.

As if alerted to his presence, she raised her head. Desire shimmered in the depth of her eyes, then faded behind a mask of uncertainty. "Hello."

"Should I assume you're here because you like football?" he asked pointedly.

"No." Her voice came out in a whisper. She picked at the pretzel, absently flicking off the chunks of salt. "I wanted to talk to you."

"Could you have picked a more public place?"

"I didn't plan it like this."

"How did you plan it?"

She hunched her shoulders. "Okay, so maybe I didn't plan it at all."

Leah had actually done something spontaneous? He was tempted to check her temperature and make sure she didn't have a fever.

"Would you rather I leave?" she asked.

"Is that what you want?"

"If I knew what I wanted, you wouldn't be mad at me now, would you?"

He couldn't argue with her twisted logic. Getting her to admit what she wanted was only half the problem—she had to face her feelings instead of running away from them. Before he could help her, he needed to understand the root of her fears.

"Do you want to stay for the rest of the game?" He pointed toward the field.

"Is this a trick question?"

"What does that mean?"

"If I say yes, you'll accuse me of stalling. If I say no, I've ruined your plans for the evening."

"Will you take a stand and stick to it?" He groaned. "Pretend you're at work—you never have a problem being decisive there."

"I want to stay." She raised her chin defiantly and strolled toward the bleachers.

"Coward," he muttered with a laugh. She whirled around and sent him a look. There *was* hope for her.

Leah folded her hands in her lap and leaned back into the sofa. An uncomfortable silence settled over the room. She had apologized. Jack had shrugged. Perhaps she should have chosen a neutral place. In his house, he had a major advantage over her.

Get a reality check, Leah. Even in your house he'd have a huge advantage over you.

He lowered himself into a chair at the opposite end of the room. She understood the message his physical distance represented. This time, she was in the dog house.

"I don't know what you want from me, Jack."

"Maybe we should start with what *you* want from me. Despite the irony of our relationship, I will not be content to sit around and wait for a few moments of your spare time."

"That's hardly fair. I work fourteen hours a day, sometimes seven days a week. What am I supposed to do?"

"For now, I'd be content if you would let

me take on more responsibility at work so that you would have more free time."

"To spend with you?" she asked.

He tipped his head. "Do you want a relationship with me or not?"

"Yes . . . and no." She clenched her fingers together. "I do want to be with you. But I'm scared."

His expression softened. He moved to the seat next to her, but gently pushed her away when she tried to snuggle closer. "No."

Again, his message was clear: if she wasn't ready to make a commitment, he didn't want a relationship.

"Tell me what you're afraid of." He never asked simple questions.

"For one thing, I haven't a clue what it's like to be in a relationship."

"You've had family relationships. It's no different."

Family? The closest thing she had to a family was the cooking staff at the school cafeteria where she ate her meals alone in the kitchen. At night *The Partridge Family* and *Nancy Drew* kept her company.

"My mother died when I was born, and looking back, my father died along with her.

His body just went on for another twenty-five years."

Twenty-five years of blaming and punishing his only child for living. A hollow ache settled in her chest. Strangely, she had thought that the memories couldn't hurt her anymore. But how could they not, when the past still ruled the way she dealt with the present?

"Are you okay?"

She nodded and took a deep breath. "When I was a little girl, I used to think that I killed my mother, so God punished me by making me invisible. That's why my father couldn't see me."

"He probably didn't know how to deal with his grief."

"I can't ever remember him holding me or saying one word of encouragement." Her father had showed more concern and affection for his players than he ever had for her. "There were times when I really believed he hated me, and other times when I would have welcomed a display of any emotion—including hate."

"What about the aunt that you visit every week?"

"Aunt Mary was my mother's sister. My

father had no use for her, so I didn't get to see much of her until I started college in the city." By that time, she had already built a fortress around her emotions. Her childhood left a void that she had never allowed anyone to fill. "The closest I ever had to a father figure was Edward Rockford. But then my dear old dad, with his wondrous paternalistic instincts, assumed that I had to be sleeping with Edward. How else would I be making so much money?"

Jack closed his hand over her clenched fist and softly stroked her wrist. "Maybe he was jealous of your feelings for Mr. Rockford."

"He was jealous of my *success*. Most parents want their children to have a better life than they had. He didn't. He just wanted me to pay for living when my mother had died."

"I can imagine it was horrible, but you survived and you're stronger because of it."

"Am I?" she asked pointedly. "Then why do I always seem to date men who don't want to give anything of themselves?"

He shook his head. "I don't know."

"I can answer that: women seek out men like their fathers."

"I'm nothing like that," he said defensively.

A sad smile tugged at the corner of her mouth. "And that's why you scare me. We're completely different. You like confrontation, I prefer retreat. You're demonstrative, I get embarrassed by displays of affection."

"And you're a girl and I'm a boy," he said lightly, pointing out how silly her argument sounded. "That's why nature planned for opposites to attract."

She expelled an exasperated sigh. "I'm not making myself clear."

"You're very clear Leah, but so far you haven't given me one good reason. If you love me, then the differences can be worked out. And if you don't, well . . ."

"I do," she whispered. *How could he think otherwise?*

"I'm sorry." He tapped his ear. "I didn't catch that."

"I said I do love you." She gazed up at him. Her mouth went dry. The half inch between them seemed like a mile. "Am I allowed to touch you yet?"

Jack let out a laugh. "For someone who isn't demonstrative, you certainly are impatient to snuggle up. We still have a few details to work out."

"Details? You have no idea what you'd be letting yourself in for."

Jack smiled at her warning. "Why don't you tell me."

"As girlfriend material, I'm no bargain. I can't cook. No one will ever mistake me for Susie Homemaker, and when I'm in a bad mood, you don't want to be within a five mile radius."

He brushed his mouth over her lips, then said, "I can cook. I'm not looking for someone to take care of me, and when you're in a bad mood I'll turn you loose on my little brother."

"I'm probably going to be tougher on you at work because I'll be afraid to show bias." She twisted beneath him, trying to crack his single minded control.

"I'll learn more, faster. Are you out of excuses yet?"

"Either that, or out of patience." She pulled her hands free and wrapped her arms around his waist.

"Was that a yes or a no?" he asked.

"All right, we'll give it a try."

"Good." He rose from the sofa.

Her eyes widened in surprise. A chill replaced the warmth his body had provided.

"Um, excuse me, but weren't we in the middle of something here?"

Jack ignored her. "Now, tomorrow . . . Darn, tomorrow I promised to help my aunt paint her living room. No matter. You can take my Jeep and pick up your clothes. We'll deal with the furniture later."

His pressure to settle the arrangements immediately left her wondering what she had let herself in for. Despite his claim that he had no problem with her being the boss at work, he seemed determined to be in total control away from the office. "Jack, you're taking a lot of things for granted."

"You said yes."

She closed her fingers over his arm and gave him a squeeze. "To a relationship. Not to moving in here just yet." He didn't look happy, but he didn't seem angry either. "And I would appreciate keeping this quiet at work for a while. Let me get used to the idea before I have to defend myself for being a hypocrite."

Something flickered in his eyes, then disappeared as he nodded. "All right." His agreement was half-hearted.

"You want me to turn my whole life upside down. I'm sorry if I'm not doing it fast enough for your liking."

He pushed his fingers into her hair. His uncertain smile relieved a few of her own doubts. "I'm only asking you to trust me."

"You're asking me to go from living alone to sharing a house with you, your younger brother and a boa constrictor. There's a little bit more than trust involved here."

"Okay. We'll take things slower." She wasn't sure Jack knew the meaning of taking things slow, but he was willing to meet her halfway in all areas of their relationship. She could do no less.

Jack pulled on a pair of sweatpants and staggered down the stairs. Sounds from the kitchen halted him. Either Tim was up or Leah had arrived. Although why she had insisted on returning to her apartment last night when he had an empty one downstairs, was beyond him. He peered into the room and smiled. Leah hadn't lied when she said she couldn't cook. Two slices of jet black toast popped from the toaster, setting off the smoke detector. Frantically, she waved a towel in front of the alarm until the annoying beep stopped.

She turned, saw him and spun back around. "Go away."

"The toaster doesn't work too well."

"I suppose the frying pan is broken too?" She gestured toward the bacon that looked more like beef jerky. "Should I even attempt the eggs?"

"Scramble them," he offered helpfully. "It's kind of hard to mess up."

"If there's a way, I will."

"Where's Tim?"

"He went out right after I got here."

Jack stepped into the kitchen. "I'll give you a hand."

She ran a sweeping gaze along the length of him. The corners of her mouth lifted in a grin. "That will help my concentration."

Her smile touched him as much as her unsuccessful effort to make breakfast. She looked adorable in a pair of soft denim jeans and a *New York Giants* football jersey. Her toes, with their pink painted nails, wiggled against the linoleum floor as she shifted her weight from foot to foot.

Having Leah in his kitchen was a sight he definitely liked—he didn't care if she could cook.

He pulled her into an embrace and pushed

her hair back from her face. Her breath caught in her throat. The front door opened and hit the wall with a resounding crash. Like a child about to get caught with her hand in the cookie jar, she squirmed to free herself from his embrace.

"It's Tim." He groaned in disappointment. "He'll have to get used to seeing us like this."

"Don't you think you should tell him first?" The hint of concern in her voice made him smile.

"I think he already suspects it."

"Yo. Anybody home?" The baritone voice didn't belong to Tim.

Leah tensed in his arms. When she had asked him not to make their relationship public knowledge, he had forgotten that Randy had a tendency to make himself at home.

"I have to start locking the door."

"Hey, Jack. I'm really sorry about yesterday. I hope I didn't ruin your . . ." Randy walked into the kitchen and stopped in his tracks. ". . . evening plans."

Just his morning plans, Leah thought.

She had known her life would change radically when she agreed to get involved with Jack. Randy had not been part of the deal.

So much for keeping their relationship quiet. The BBC had learned the art of rapid communication from Randy. She glanced over her shoulder at the shocked expression on her coworker's face.

"Good morning," she said cheerfully.

For the first time since she had known him, Randy was speechless.

She twisted out of Jack's arms. As she smoothed her clothes, she silently cursed the compromising position she had been caught in. She couldn't pass this off as a working weekend. Thankfully, Randy was too stunned to make a crass comment. In her present mood, she wouldn't be held responsible for her actions. "If you'll excuse me, I have to powder my nose or something."

Randy's stunned gaze followed Leah until she ascended the stairs. "Well, this is an interesting turn of events. How did you manage to thaw the Ice Queen?"

Jack wanted to wipe the nasty smirk off his friend's face. Instead, he changed the subject. "Would you mind knocking before you come in from now on?"

"Why? Is she going to be around here often?"

"That's not the point. And it's none of your business."

"A woman in the last bastion of male territory?" Randy placed his hand across his chest in mock-horror. "What does Tim think about this?"

"I don't think he'll have a problem." Unlike Randy, who seemed to be quite agitated.

"What happened to you? You've turned into your father. You've got the little woman. What's next? A station wagon to run to the P.T.A. meetings?"

Jack couldn't help but feel sorry for his friend. At twenty-nine, Randy still thought and behaved like an adolescent. "Is there something wrong with spending time with a woman?"

Randy shrugged and poured himself a cup of coffee. "Not just any woman—*Ms. Matthews*. I thought you had a thing against sleeping with the boss to get ahead."

"Drop it before you say something stupid. Whatever is running through that twisted mind of yours is way off the mark. And I won't have you talking about her in that way."

"Oh, come on. You've all but said she'll be living here."

"I said she would be spending *time* here," Jack corrected. "And I'd like to keep it quiet at work, if you don't mind."

"You can trust me," Randy assured him.

"Sure." Jack knew it was only a matter of time before his friend would *slip*. Whoever said that only women gossip had never worked in an office

"Although . . ." Randy's lip curled back in a lop-sided grin. "I'd love to be a fly on the wall when Ellen finds out. As it is, she's always been jealous of Leah's friendship with her father and her ex-husband. Now she's taken you, too. It could be a heck of a cat-fight."

Jack groaned. He could only hope that Ellen would let the matter rest. Legally, she couldn't fire him because he wasn't interested in her, but she didn't like to lose. He remembered her fury when Marcus Chatsworth had mentioned offering Leah a job. "Let's hope she doesn't hear any time soon."

Chapter Nine

On Monday morning, Leah came down with an acute case of paranoia. Had Randy sent her a friendly smile or a knowing smirk? Were her coworkers fishing for personal information or simply asking about her weekend? And what was the big deal about her wearing a red dress, anyway? Why had three people felt the need to point it out?

If she kept this up, she would have ulcers within the week. She craved a cup of strong coffee, but opted instead for weak tea.

Leah entered the break room. A group of women huddled together, giggling like schoolgirls. Between them, a magazine was being pulled in all directions.

"What's so interesting?"

A guilty silence fell over the room. The magazine was snapped shut, and Sue held it behind her back.

"Nothing. Just an article," her assistant said.

"It must be good. Let me see."

Sue exchanged glances with her friends and reluctantly handed over the periodical, a three-year-old copy of *Sports Illustrated*. The page was dog-eared, but Leah suspected the magazine would have opened to that place on its own.

She tried not to show any emotion as she ogled the picture of Jack, wearing a skimpy track outfit with the red, white and blue insignia of the American team. His gold medal hung around his neck, and he wore running sneakers that some company had apparently paid him to endorse.

"Well?" Sue asked.

"Well." Leah paused. *He looks much better in person.* "It's a nice picture. Well-balanced and visual. It sells the product, but why anyone would pay one hundred dollars for sneakers is beyond me."

Megan, from accounting, shook her head. "The athlete, Ms. Matthews. Did you happen to notice him?"

"I'd have to be asleep not to." She exhaled a sigh of appreciation, then closed the magazine and returned it to Sue. "Where did this come from?"

"Randy gave it to me," Megan supplied happily.

"That was very considerate of him." Leah forced herself to smile. Too bad Randy hadn't considered the feelings of his friend before passing around something from Jack's past that he wasn't looking to play up. "Although, I think it's more productive to review *Vogue* if you're looking for trends in the fashion industry."

"You weren't in the least bit interested in something besides the sneakers in that ad?" Sue asked.

"Actually . . . I was impressed with the graphic lay out, too." A collective sigh of hopelessness echoed through the break room. They'd given Leah up as a lost cause. She filled her cup with boiling water and dunked a tea bag inside. "I'll see you later."

"Leah," Megan said, halting her exit.

Leah turned back. "Yes?"

"Does he look as good without the track suit on?"

Every ounce of strength she could muster went into holding her tea cup, and herself, upright. Apparently Randy, in his endeavors to impress the lovely young Megan, had been running on at the mouth. His promise to remain quiet lasted a whopping forty-eight hours. And even then, he couldn't get the facts right.

"Leah?" Sue's voice was a combination of shock and envy. "Are you holding out on us?"

Was *this* the female camaraderie she had thought her life lacked? Being on the receiving end wasn't the fun she had imagined.

"I'll never tell." She waltzed out the door.

Her ego, flying high, took a nose dive when she heard someone mumble, "I hope her health insurance is paid when Ms. Rockford finds out."

Until now, Leah hadn't given that eventuality a thought. Since the Gabriel Benefit, Ellen hadn't been in the office. Not that she was missed, but Leah knew it wasn't a good sign. Ellen handled rejection the way she handled the aging process—with a vengeance.

* * *

Leah arrived at the restaurant a few minutes early. The call from Marcus had been a welcome surprise. In the rush of the past few weeks she had forgotten about their brief meeting in Atlanta. As she stepped inside the door, she saw him already waiting at the bar.

With his usual pace-setting speed, he whisked her to the table and spelled out his offer before they had ordered dinner. Marcus had once told her that etiquette was for people with too much time or too much money, and he had neither.

"It will be like old times, Leah. Jerry is running the accounting department, and Tom's heading up sales."

She smiled. Marcus had made a habit of hiring ex-Rockford employees—particularly those with a grudge against Ellen. Although she was the first person, to her knowledge, that he had attempted to recruit while still on Rockford's payroll.

Marcus drummed his fingers impatiently on the table.

"Can I think about it over dinner?" she asked.

"What's to think about? If it's a matter of money, we can negotiate."

"It's not the money."

"You don't want to work in Atlanta? Work out of the New York office."

She shook her head sadly. "That's not it. I promised Edward I would stay until Ellen could run the company herself. He was like a father to me."

"Me too, Leah," Marcus said softly. "The only one who didn't feel that way about him was his daughter. You've honored that promise for five years, and she's done nothing but make your life a misery because of it. It's going to get worse, not better."

Leah had no qualms about walking out on Ellen. Two months ago she would have jumped at the chance. Two months ago she wasn't in love with a man who, with just a glance, could make her heart soar. "I can't answer right this minute."

"Is there some other reason you want to stay?"

"Like what?" she asked.

"Like who, you mean. You're seeing someone from the office and you're worried about a conflict of interest."

She wasn't sure if he possessed amazing

insight or hired remarkable spies, but he had narrowed in on the core of her concern with uncanny precision. "You're too smart for your own good."

He grinned. "I don't have a problem. Work is work and personal is personal. I know you'll keep the two separate."

"I'll think about it. That's all I can promise right now."

And think about it, she did. On the bus ride to New Jersey, she thought of nothing else. Would Ellen be as open-minded as her ex-husband? *Sure, Leah. And you still believe in Santa Claus too.*

Leah walked in the door and dropped her briefcase in the nearest chair. She hadn't planned to be this late. At least she made it to his house before the start of the football game. Tim was sprawled out on the sofa in front of the television. When he saw her, he hit the mute button. "You're here."

"Where's Jack?"

"He said he was going out running, but he's really looking for you. He was afraid you missed your bus stop." Tim chuckled.

She didn't know whether to laugh or smack Jack in the head when he returned. He had told her she was brilliant, yet he thought her incapable of finding her way to his house past eight o'clock. She kicked off her shoes and flopped down in a chair.

"Should I go look for him?" Tim asked.

"Nah. Let him sweat." Ten minutes later, when she heard the Jeep pull into the driveway, she grabbed her shoes and briefcase. "Shhh," she said.

"You're rotten," he said with a grin. "Too bad my brother found you first."

"Bless you. If I were fifteen years younger . . ." She sprinted up the stairs as the front door opened.

"Did she call?" Jack asked nervously.

Tim shrugged. "No."

Jack glanced at his watch. It was still early. She probably ended up staying for dinner after her meeting. No, she wouldn't have done that without calling first. She carried a cellular phone in her purse.

"What could have happened?" he wondered aloud.

"Aliens kidnapped her?" Tim offered helpfully.

"Funny."

"Maybe she's discovered the real you and she's never coming back."

"Shut up before I ground you."

"For what?"

"Breathing," Jack shot back.

"Don't yell at him, you big grouch," Leah said as she came down the stairs. She pointed to her watch and frowned. "Eight-fifteen, Jack. Where have you been at this hour? Tim and I were worried sick. Try to call if you're going to be later than eight o'clock."

Jack glared at his brother. "Why didn't you tell me she was here?"

Tim's blue eyes widened innocently. "You didn't ask *that*."

"You're enjoying this, aren't you?"

"Yep. And I think Leah is, too."

He glanced at her. Sure enough, she was enjoying his uncharacteristic display of anxiety. A small giggle escaped from her pouting lips and her eyes shimmered with amusement.

Jack threw his hands up in the air. He couldn't help himself. Worrying about Leah was a natural extension of his paternal relationship with his brother. "So, shoot me."

"No. We'll keep you around for a while." She stepped into his arms and kissed him.

"Oh, jeez." Tim sprung to his feet. "If you guys are gonna be lip-locked all night, I'm watching the game in my room."

Leah let out a groan. A scarlet flush covered her face as she tried to wiggle out of his arms. Apparently she only enjoyed the teenage abuse when Jack was the target.

Once they were alone, she settled down on the sofa next to him, but her mind wasn't on *Monday Night Football*. Her home team, the Giants, didn't gain a moment of her attention, even when they scored a brilliant touchdown.

He brushed his knuckles over her cheek. "Did something go wrong with your meeting?"

"No, the meeting went well."

"Then what's up?"

She took a deep breath and said, "Marcus Chatsworth offered me a job today." The words spilled out with breathless relief.

"Oh," he managed. His previous meeting with the man was still fresh in his mind. Although he didn't like the idea of Leah working for Marcus, he kept his opinion to himself. "What did you say?"

She snuggled up against him. "I told him I would think about it."

"A good job?"

"Vice president."

"Big raise?"

"That too."

"So, what's to think about?"

She exhaled slowly. "Gee, Jack, I don't know. Twice as much travel. Weeks at a time in Atlanta, where the company is based. And you."

"Don't use me as an excuse. You have to make your own decision based on what's best for you, not me."

"What about what's best for *us*?"

"What do you want?"

"I want you to tell me not to take it," she said with simple honesty.

He wanted to tell her the same thing, but how could he? She deserved everything Marcus Chatsworth offered. No one worked harder than she did, and she wasn't compensated in her present position. "I can't. That wouldn't be fair."

"I was afraid you'd say that."

Apparently, she was leaning toward declining the offer. With a stab of guilt, he acknowledged that he was the main reason. Still, he remained silent.

He eased her head onto his shoulder pressed a kiss against her temple. All those insecurities that Leah believed he didn't possess, hovered just below the surface. He should have showed more enthusiasm and support for an offer he would have killed for. No doubt Ellen would expect him to cover Leah's position, but Ellen had no idea how much responsibility Leah shouldered at Rockford Industries. The marketing end he could cover, but marketing was one-tenth of what Leah did for the company.

In truth, he didn't want her to leave, and it had nothing to do with his job. The thought of Leah spending weeks on the road made him downright uncomfortable. When had he developed such a possessive nature?

After two blissful weeks of calm, Ms. Rockford returned to the office. Anticipation of a showdown between her and Leah made for much quiet speculation around the break room. A series of meetings had kept Leah out of the path of the storm, but shortly after lunch Hurricane Ellen blew into her office.

"I understand you're planning to leave," Ellen said. She planted her hands on her hips and clicked a stiletto heel against the floor.

Leah shrugged and absently straightened the papers on her desk. "Then you know something I don't."

"I happen to know you met with Marcus while you were in Atlanta last month."

"I ran into him," she corrected.

"I'm sure it was no accident." Ellen's voice rang with bitter accusation.

"Is there a company policy against speaking to a former colleague?"

She let out a shrill laugh. "You're not big on company policy lately."

Leah met Ellen's cold glare with one of her own. "Meaning?"

"Weren't you the one who got on a soapbox and preached about intercompany affairs?"

"It's not a company policy." How could she enforce a rule that the acting president didn't adhere to?

Ellen arched a tweezed eyebrow. "Or a personal one, it seems."

"My personal life is none of your business. If you have a problem with my work, I'd be happy to address that issue."

"Don't play games. I know Marcus made you an offer. He's not the only one with spies."

Of that, Leah had no doubt. The way Ellen and Marcus spied on each other could put the CIA to shame.

"He made an offer. I didn't accept."

"Maybe you should."

Leah nodded. "Maybe I will."

"Then I'll expect your resignation on my desk by the end of the day."

Instead of the guilt and sorrow she had expected to feel, relief spread through her, as if a suffocating weight had been lifted. "Thank you for making it so easy."

"I told you. No one is irreplaceable." Ellen turned and stood in the doorway for a long moment. Her frigid stare reflected a cruel glint. "Oh, and one more thing."

"I'm sure there is."

"Your relationship with Jackson Brandt . . ."

"Is none of your business," Leah cut in quickly and sprung to her feet. "I no longer work for you."

"Oh, but *he* does. I'm sure you're aware of the conflict of interest. Particularly in an industry that's so highly competitive." Ellen paused and waved her arm for dramatic effect. "Or maybe he'll be content to stay home and let you support him and little Tim."

"How did you . . ." Leah began before she could stop herself.

"Randy can be a fountain of information.

I'm surprised you haven't noticed his potential before."

Randy? Leah wondered if Randy had deliberately attempted to hurt Jack, or if he had wanted to hurt *her*. The latter seemed more likely, but why? "Jack is good. He'll find another job."

"It doesn't look good on a résumé to be fired from a job after two months. Particularly if the reason was his attempt to seduce his way up the corporate ladder."

Leah couldn't hold back. "You're a witch."

"I know." Ellen smiled proudly. "You won over my father and my husband. But this time the witch is going to win."

"You'll never have him. He's got something your money can't buy. Pride."

"Pride doesn't pay the mortgage. And even if you're right, you won't have him either."

"You'd do this to the company just to get back at me? I didn't realize you found me that big of a threat."

Ellen snorted, and Leah could have sworn that fire came out. "I think you overestimate your importance to me and the company."

"We'll see." Leah held the door open for

Ellen's exit. "If you'll excuse me, I have to call Marcus and tell him I accept the position. Should I send him your regards?"

Ellen blew out of the office on the same gale force she had entered. The clicking of her heels echoed down the corridor, followed by the thunderous crashing of her office door slamming shut.

Finally, the anxiety of the past two weeks was over. The rush of relief and excitement lasted only a few short seconds before the reality of her situation set in. She slumped against the wall and exhaled slowly.

What would she say to Jack? If she told him the truth, he would most likely quit. She didn't want to be responsible for him being unemployed while she had a new and better position.

Working from New York wasn't a viable option, because she could never explain to him why she couldn't see him anymore. His friend Randy wouldn't keep his mouth shut if she stayed, and Ellen would find out and fire Jack for spite.

Leah refused to concede defeat. She would beat Ellen. If she spent the first six months working from Atlanta, Jack would have time to make himself indispensable to Rockford.

He was probably the last person left who could keep the company running. In that time he would build his résumé. If he was forced to resign when she returned, he would have no trouble finding a new position.

She raked a handful of hair away from her face and sighed. Her planned scenario took too much for granted.

The other possibility tied her stomach in knots. Would he wait for her to return, even though she couldn't tell him the whole truth? She had proven, on more than one occasion, that she preferred retreat rather than confrontation. Would he view her defection as desertion? She tried to have more faith in their love, but years of insecurity plagued her.

Chapter Ten

Jack snapped the lock on his briefcase. One month down, five to go. Time would probably pass more quickly if the office staff didn't treat him like a refugee from a leper colony. Granted, he hadn't stopped Leah from leaving, but the decision to move to Atlanta had been hers alone.

Dealing with the black widow in the corner office was bad enough. He was running out of excuses to avoid her business lunches. Ellen played the part of the wounded party to perfection, but Jack got the feeling that she hadn't shed any tears over Leah's departure.

At least not while things were running smoothly.

He shut off the computer and straightened the papers on his desk. Silence mocked him from every corridor. When counting paper clips seemed like an exciting alternative to returning to an empty house, he knew he was in for a long weekend. Since Tim had a break in the football schedule, he had decided to go camping with his cousins. And who could blame him? Jack couldn't stand his own company—how could he expect anyone else to?

"Hey, Jack. I'm glad I caught you." Randy came into his office.

"You need a ride home?" Jack asked.

"Heck no. I came to get you. Megan brought her sister to Murphy's, and she's one fine-looking babe."

Babe. That would have earned him a swift kick in the shins from Leah, Jack thought. "Not interested."

"Why not? You lost the ball and chain. You're a free agent."

"I haven't *lost* Leah. She's in Atlanta to get things running so she can work from New York. She'll be back in six months."

"You'd better hope not, or you'll lose your job too."

"What are you talking about?"

"A little thing called 'conflict of interest', pal. She works for the competition now. You don't think Ellen would keep you if she thought you were still seeing Leah, do you?"

Jack shook his head. "That's ridiculous."

"You think so? Then why did Ellen demand Leah's resignation? I'll tell you why. She found out your girlfriend was meeting with Marcus Chatsworth."

"Leah resigned for a better position."

"Not according to Ellen."

Jack raised an eyebrow at the positive note in Randy's voice. "Is she your bosom buddy now?"

"We talk from time to time." Randy leaned against the wall. "Don't blow it, man. No woman is worth your job. Especially when there's another one waiting down the street."

"Are you telling me that Ellen fired Leah?"

Apparently annoyed with the continued conversation, Randy sniped, "Wow, the man *is* quick. I guess that's why you're a gold-medal runner."

Jack had gotten the distinct impression that Leah planned to turn down the offer with Mercury. The guilt he carried over his lack of support for her had stopped him from questioning her change of heart. Now he couldn't help but wonder what Ellen had said that had pushed Leah into resigning.

Conflict of interest.

Since Randy was loyal to no one, he couldn't have come up with the concept on his own. Had Leah accepted the offer in Atlanta to save him his job? That was something she would do. Especially if his *good friend* Randy had given Ellen enough information to push the right buttons.

"Are you coming?" Randy asked impatiently.

Without answering, Jack grabbed his briefcase and stormed out of his office. Although it was after six, Sue was still at her desk.

"Do you have a few minutes?" Jack asked.

She glared at him. "You're the boss."

"I want you to type up my resignation. It shouldn't take too long. Just use the same letter you used for Leah, and insert my name."

"Have you completely lost your mind?" Randy bellowed from behind him.

For the first time since he started at Rockford, Sue smiled at him. "I think he just found it."

"Don't do this." Randy grasped at Jack's sleeve. "I went out on a limb to recommend you for this job. My reputation is at stake."

Jack stepped back. "Oh, good. Then you won't be losing too much. And Randy, don't bother stopping by the house. I doubt Leah would want to see you."

Leah kicked off her shoes by the door. One month of living in an impersonal hotel room had been four weeks too many, but she couldn't bring herself to rent an apartment. As long as she stayed in the hotel she could convince herself that the situation was temporary.

Time had not eased the loneliness she felt. Jack had been so darned understanding about her leaving. Perhaps if he had gotten angry she wouldn't feel so guilty about her half-truths and evasions. She spoke to him twice a week, but the clear fiber optic connection lacked the warmth of his presence.

She missed him. She hadn't imagined that

twenty-eight days could pass so slowly. *Every pain is a learning experience,* she reminded herself. So far, the only lesson she had learned during the separation was that she didn't want to be alone anymore.

Jack glanced around the darkened restaurant. His Jeep was packed, and he would have been halfway down the New Jersey Turnpike by now if not for the strange message he had received on his answering machine. Although he had no idea why Marcus Chatsworth wanted to speak with him, he was intrigued enough to hold off his departure to Atlanta a few hours.

As if their last meeting had never occurred, Marcus rose from the table with a big grin and offered his hand in a friendly welcome. "I'm glad you made it. I wasn't sure if you'd show up."

Jack shook his hand. "I almost didn't." He wouldn't have, except the man was Leah's boss. If Marcus had news about her, Jack wanted to know before driving all night to see her.

"I guess you know why I called."

"Actually, I don't."

Marcus looked amused. "Then why are you here?"

"Curiosity, I guess."

"Have a seat." He gestured toward an empty chair and waited for Jack to sit. "It's no secret that I have been known to hire qualified people who have experience in the industry. It has come to my attention that you recently resigned from Rockford."

Jack squared his jaw to keep from looking like a human fly catcher. The ink had barely dried on his resignation. How could this man know, when Ellen Rockford probably hadn't even seen the letter yet?

"You seem surprised," Marcus noted.

"Our last meeting wasn't what I'd call cordial," Jack reminded him.

Marcus bowed his head. "It doesn't happen often, but occasionally I'm wrong."

"How did you hear that I was leaving?"

"I have my spies." Pride deepened the older man's voice.

Spies? Mind readers more likely. Only Randy and Sue knew. Sue, of course. She must have called Leah. "Does Leah have anything to do with this offer?"

"Leah Matthews?" Marcus drew his bushy brows together in confusion. "I haven't told her yet, but I don't imagine she'll have a problem. You've worked together before. If you didn't know your business you wouldn't have lasted one week working with her."

"So she doesn't know?" Jack asked.

"There's no point in mentioning it to her if you're not interested."

"Oh, I'm interested, but I can't relocate to Atlanta."

"I'll tell you the same thing I told Leah: you can work from here or Atlanta. The choice is yours."

"You told Leah the same thing?" Jack repeated, more to himself. So his angel had been less than honest. Why? Did she plan to remain in Atlanta permanently?

"Well?" Marcus prodded.

"You want an answer right now?"

"Any fool can explore all the angles and reach a logical conclusion. I need people who can make important decisions on gut instinct. The fine print is always negotiable later on."

"I accept. But if you don't mind, I'd prefer you didn't say anything to Leah until after I start." She had put him through four weeks of misery for nothing. Didn't she understand, that she was more important to him than any job?

Marcus grinned as if he'd just figured out the answer to a bothersome riddle. "Oh, man, how did this one slip past me?"

"Excuse me?" Jack asked.

"I knew she had been seeing *someone* from Rockford, but she never mentioned who. I gather Leah will be working from New York, after all."

Jack remained silent. The man was every bit as sharp as his reputation. Leah would be returning all right, but not before he drummed some sense into her.

Leah pushed the stop button on the VCR and collapsed into the chair. Contrary to popular belief, a strenuous work out did not relieve stress. Maybe she should take up jogging and give up the belly dancing.

A knock on her door let her know that lunch had arrived. She looked down at her less-than-attractive exercise clothes and shrugged. So, she looked like something the cat dragged in—it was her day off.

"Coming," she said on the third knock. She dragged herself up from the chair and shuffled across the floor. By the fourth knock, she pulled the door open and grumbled, "Chill out."

"You have to stop picking up your vocabulary from Tim."

"Jack?" Sure her imagination was playing tricks on her, she shook her head and blinked. His image remained. She raked her fingers though her tangled mass of curls, still damp from her work out. "Why didn't you tell me you were coming?"

"May I come in?" His voice was polite but cool. Apparently, he had more than a social call on his mind.

Her smile faded and her mouth went dry. "Sure." She stepped back and allowed him to enter.

"How have you been?" He hadn't traveled eight hundred miles to inquire about her health.

She wanted to throw herself in his arms but he seemed so distant. "I'm all right. I've missed you."

"Have you?"

Stay calm, she told herself. She was the one who had left without a full explanation. "What kind of question is that? Do you think I like this separation?"

"I'm not sure. Do you?"

She stepped toward him and put her hand on his shoulder. How she had missed the feel of him! "Surely you didn't fly all this way to pick a fight."

"Actually, I did," he said, clasping a tight grip around her wrist and removing her hand. "And I didn't fly, I drove."

No wonder he seemed so tired—and irritable, if his provocative mood was any indication. She lowered herself onto the edge of the bed. "I don't want to fight."

"I know. You'd rather run away to another state."

A sharp pain cut through her. She sucked in a large gulp of air and suppressed the urge to give him exactly what he wanted. "That's not fair."

"I know. So how come you're not getting mad?"

"It seems to me that you've got enough anger for the two of us. What did I do that brought you all the way down here?"

His blue eyes bore a hole to her soul as he stared down at her. "For starters, you lied to me about your reasons for leaving Rockford."

Leah exhaled a deep sigh. She could only imagine what Ellen had told him. Jack wasn't prone to believing rumors—he must have stumbled onto the truth. Or part of it, anyway.

"I didn't lie. I omitted a few details. Don't tell me you've never done that to me."

The reminder of their ominous beginning stopped him cold. "Touché."

She sprang to her feet and began pacing the room. Room? The large elegant suite had become a prison. A six-month term she had sentenced herself to in order to protect his job.

"I resigned because I was asked to. But I'm sure you already know that."

"You didn't have to take a job in Atlanta. I would have helped you out until you found another position."

"That's very nice. And would you have let me help *you* out if you had lost your job?" she snapped, before she could stop herself.

He arched his eyebrow. "Was there a chance of that?"

"What?"

"Is that what Ellen told you? If you didn't leave, I would lose my job?"

"No."

"No more lies, Leah."

"I'm not lying, exactly. Our relationship

was a conflict of interest with your position in the company. Accepting the job here seemed like the best short-term solution I could find."

"Did you plan to return in six months, or did you *omit* the fact that you planned to relocate here permanently?"

Leah folded her arms across her chest and raised her head to meet his glare with an icy one of her own. He had pushed her one step too far. "What is this, the inquisition?"

Jack laughed at her outburst.

Her anger amused him, causing her temper to soar even higher. "Where was all this righteous anger when I left? I didn't notice you getting bent out of shape over my departure. Maybe if you had made a scene then, you could have saved yourself the gas money driving down here now."

"I should have, now that I'm out of a job."

Leah felt the air go out of her body. "She fired you anyway?"

Jack picked up on her telltale slip. "So she did threaten you. Why didn't you tell me the truth?"

"You would have quit."

"I did anyway."

"But not because of me," she pointed out.

He cupped his hands over her shoulders and gave her a small shake. "You are so blind when it comes to me. It's always been because of you, Leah. Everything I've done. I knew that Ellen didn't hire me for my outstanding credentials almost from the beginning. I stayed for the chance to work with you, to learn from you. To prove myself to you."

The sting of salty tears filled her eyes. "You don't have to prove yourself to me."

"Apparently I do if you think that a job is more important to me than you are. I love you."

"I know. And I love you too, but there wasn't only me to consider. You have Tim . . ." Her words caught in her throat.

His expression softened. "My brother and I have been through tougher times than this. I'll find another job." He slid his hands down to her waist and pulled her to him.

"But I won't find anyone to replace you."

"No one is irreplaceable," she whispered.

"You are. I won't let you run away from me."

"I didn't run away from you. I took a leave of absence."

He gazed lovingly at her. "Well, it's time to come back."

"As soon as I can arrange it," she agreed eagerly. At that moment she was so happy, she would have agreed to anything.

"Arrange it by tomorrow. You're driving back with me."

"And what are you going to do when we get there, Jack?"

"We'll figure that out together."

Together. She liked the sound of that. He had come all this way for her. To bring her back home to him. The love she felt for him warmed her to the very core. She hadn't felt this happy, this loved . . . heck, she'd never felt *anything* until she met Jack. He had opened her heart to a world of emotions, and she would spend the rest of her life returning the favor.

Jack unfastened the button of his suit jacket and sat behind the desk in his new office. He checked his watch. Leah had set up a nine o'clock meeting with Marcus Chatsworth to discuss her reasons for returning to the New York office. Any moment Jack expected a visit.

Perhaps he should have told her about his

new position, but he didn't want anything to influence her decision to return. Although he felt a sense of déjà vu, he hoped the outcome would be better than the first time around.

Leah burst into his office a full five minutes later than he expected. Her face was flushed and her eyes narrowed. He squelched the urge to kiss the pout off her lips.

"Jackson Brandt. You did it to me again."

He couldn't tell if her anger was real or not, so he played innocent. "What did I do?"

"This." She waved her arm in a sweeping gesture around the room. "You should have told me before we left Atlanta. You know how I feel about interoffice romance."

"We're more than a romance. We're a team. Like Gable and Lombard, or Spencer and Tracy."

"Or Laurel and Hardy?" She rested against the edge of his desk and smiled. "And this is another fine mess you've gotten me into."

He shrugged and clasped his hands together behind his head. "You could fire me."

"No I can't. No grounds. You haven't messed up yet, and I don't imagine you will."

"Then there shouldn't be a problem with us working together."

"What happens if you start to think you've been treated unfairly? Next thing I know, I'm in court for sexual harassment."

His rich laugh filled the office. "Believe me. I don't think of anything you do to me as harassment in any way, shape or form."

"Yet."

"There is an answer to this personal dilemma of yours."

"What's that?"

"You could marry me. That would prevent me from being able to testify against you in this hypothetical suit."

"It would," she agreed. Was he serious or making a point of how silly she sounded?

"Is that a yes?"

"Was that a proposal?"

"Yes."

Her overly cautious conscience warned her that this was not a decision to be made without long deliberation. But when had she ever listened to her own advice where Jack was concerned?

"Yes," she said, without stopping to consider.

In the space of a heartbeat, Jack sprang out of his chair and took her in his arms. He let out a sigh of relief. How could he have doubted what her answer would be?

One kiss to celebrate the engagement, she decided. One kiss led to another, and all too soon she had forgotten all her own rules about office decorum.

"Cut it out, Jack."

"A little danger stimulates the senses. And I'd prove it to you right here and now, but I've got this boss lady who's really hung up on office propriety." His gaze swept over her, leaving her with no question that he found her beautiful. His patience with all her irrational uncertainty left her with no doubt that he loved her as well. She might be a bit of a basket case where he was concerned, but apparently, the man had a thing for baskets.

"I love you, Jack."

"I know. And I'm the luckiest guy in the world."